Praise for Travis Hunter

A ONE WOMAN MAN

"Avid Hunter readers will appreciate [*A One Woman Man*]. New readers will be fond of his edgy style and heartfelt delivery and will probably come back for more. . . . He has the uncanny ability to speak to real life situations."
—*Rolling Out*

"Hunter's dialogue is urban contemporary and quick, and the story his characters tell makes one think about the consequences that result from the choices we can make."
—*Black Issues Book Review*

"Another good Hunter novel about family love and sibling respect."
—*Booklist*

TROUBLE MAN

"Highly recommended—and y'all know I don't recommend much!"
—Eric Jerome Dickey, author of *The Other Woman*

"Once again, Travis Hunter gives us unforgettable characters that move and touch us in a way very few authors have done. *Trouble Man* is full of surprises, and it shows that, with patience, love, and a willingness to look deep within our souls, we all have the capacity to grow and change for the better. This is fabulous work from a writer who has proven once again that he's here to stay."
—Mary J. Jones, PageTurner.net

"Travis Hunter continues to deliver entertaining, funny, true-to-life stories with his latest, *Trouble Man,* a novel about love, war, family, and people struggling to do the right thing. I felt that I knew these people."
—Malik Yoba, actor and playwright

W9-ADK-200

"Travis Hunter offers insight into the male psyche in ways that will captivate the reader, with stories that are both entertaining and compelling. There is a truth and boldness to his words that make him a noteworthy force in a new generation of fiction writers."

—Lolita Files, bestselling author of *Child of God*

"Despite its title, *Married but Still Looking* is about the sanctity of marriage, accepting responsibility for one's actions and understanding the consequences of bad choices. . . . [Hunter is] a good storyteller. . . . Readers are given solid, positive messages. . . . There's a lifetime of messages in these pages." —*The Dallas Morning News*

"An honest and multidimensional portrait of a self-centered player and his entourage, framed by the crooked consequences of his own indiscretions . . . a fast and appealing read, thanks in part to the authentic characterization of Genesis . . . His struggle is genuine and familiar, and yet his actions are unpredictable." —aalbc.com

"The novel brings [Genesis Styles] and a handful of other characters . . . to understand that they can accept responsibility as lovers and parents only when they have worked through the consequences of their parents' failings. Growing up means having the faith, and the conviction, to be better lovers and better parents to the next generation."

—*The Washington Post*

"Hunter's writing is fluid and fast, and the dialogue is often raw and gritty yet comical." —*Black Issues Book Review*

"Entertaining yet enlightening . . . Travis Hunter holds the reader hostage in his thought-provoking debut. Be prepared to laugh and cry as you examine *The Hearts of Men*."

—E. Lynn Harris, author of *A Love of My Own*

"Travis Hunter takes us into the lives, the thoughts, and straight to the hearts of men. His work reflects the voice that is often missing—the voice of a brother who loves, listens, and tells his own truth."

—Bertice Berry, author of *Jim and Louella's Homemade Heart-Fix Remedy*

"A book I'll share with my sons for years to come."

—Carl Weber, author of *Baby Momma Drama*

"This moving novel . . . is insightful, sensitive and impressively real. . . ."

—*Essence*

"True-to-life debut novel. Tough lessons and father-wit loom large in this story about men staying the course and stumbling along the way."

—*Black Issues Book Review*

"Interesting and revealing look into the male psyche."

—*Today's Black Woman*

"Even cynical readers may be won over by his relentless positive message and push for African American communities built on respect and love."

—*Publishers Weekly*

"Hunter is a fresh new talent and his book, *The Hearts of Men,* gives us a glimpse into the mysterious void where black men hide their expectations, inspirations, disappointments and dreams—a place they rarely share with anyone."

—*The St. Louis American*

A Family Sin

TRAVIS HUNTER

A Family Sin

a novel

ONE WORLD / BALLANTINE BOOKS

New York

A One World Books Trade Paperback Original

Copyright © 2007 by Travis Hunter

Published in the United States by One World Books,
an imprint of The Random House Publishing Group,
a division of Random House, Inc., New York.

ONE WORLD is a registered trademark and the One World
colophon is a trademark of Random House, Inc.

LIBRARY OF CONGRESS CATALOGING-IN-PUBLICATION DATA
Hunter, Travis
A family sin : a novel / Travis Hunter.
p. cm.
"A One World Books trade paperback original."
ISBN-13: 978-0-345-48168-9 (pbk.)
1. African American families—Fiction. 2. False imprisonment—Fiction. I. Title.
PS3558.U497F36 2007
813'.54—dc22   2007020724

Printed in the United States of America

www.oneworldbooks.net

2 4 6 8 9 7 5 3 1

Book design by Casey Hampton

This book is dedicated to Rashaad and Blake

Acknowledgments

Well, well, well, here we are again. It seems like just yesterday that I sat down to try my hand at writing a novel. I cannot believe we are up to book number six. Yes, I said "we" because without the support of my friends, family, and business associates none of this would have been possible. I must start by thanking God for His continued blessings. Rashaad Hunter, my son, for making me smile every day: You are truly a blessing to my life. Linda J. Hunter, my mom, for being you. Dr. Carolyn B. Rogers, your support and encouragement never fails. Carrie Mae Moses, Sharon Capers, Andrea and David Gilmore, Barry, Ray, Gervane, Ron, Lynette, Amado, Hunter, Tony (RIP), and Louis Johnson, my dad. Ahmed Johnson, the best little bro a guy could ask for, Ayinde, Shani, and Jabadi. Ellis Sullivan, Errol Lampkin, Mary and Willard Jones, Pam and Ruffus Williams, Peggy and Steve Hicks. Tracy Bell, you won girl. Melody Guy, you are a gem. Brian McLendon, KaTrina Leon, Linda Taylor and the Sista's Sippen Tea. My agent, Sara Camilli. Moe Kelly, Shemika Turner, Yolanda Cutino, Donna King. My brothers from a different mother: Eric Jerome Dickey and Jihad. R. M. Johnson, E. Lynn Harris, Kim Roby, Kendra Norman Bellamy, Willie and Schnell Martin and the wonderful people of the Hearts of Men Foundation.

A Family Sin

1

The alarm clock beeped, waking Karim out of a dead sleep. He was never a morning person, but he couldn't take any more of the mechanical screaming. He moved his son's tiny feet from his forehead and reached over and slapped at the clock. He closed his eyes again but the alarm screamed again. He sat up and stared at the electronic aggravator as if his gaze alone would put an end to the madness.

"Baby," Lisa, his girlfriend and mother of his four-year-old son, said as she walked into the room and turned off the alarm. "It's time to get up. One more snooze and you'll be late for work."

"Who came up with that?" Karim said, frowning at the clock. "That's a horrible way to wake somebody up. Just jarring you awake like that can't be good for the heart."

"When I had it on radio, you slept right through it," Lisa said, sitting down beside him.

Karim ran his eyes over his woman's curvy figure. Her thick runner's legs, smooth chocolate skin, and nice plump breasts were his kryptonite.

Lisa caught him staring. "You see something you like?" she asked.

"Of course I do. And if I didn't have this headache you might be in trouble," he said, lying back down on the bed.

"Men," Lisa said, punching him on the leg as she jumped up from the bed. "You know they say if a man goes out and comes home drunk and won't make love to his woman that he's cheating."

"I *was* cheating," Karim said, rubbing his throbbing head at the temples. "With this little short lady named Patrón."

"Why are you drinking so much?" Lisa asked, obviously unaffected by the slight.

"I don't know."

"Leo had to drag you in here last night like some old alcoholic. I don't like that," she said, shaking her head.

"I know," Karim moaned.

He had heard this speech before, and unfortunately he was beginning to hear it a little too much.

"Well, you better get up," Lisa said, moving on with her morning rituals. "If you don't want to be late for work again."

Karim closed his eyes and massaged his temples.

"Karim," Lisa called from the bathroom.

"Yeah."

"You wanna talk?"

"About what?"

"Anything."

"Nothing to talk about," Karim lied.

Lisa sighed and walked out of the bathroom and over to the bed. She reached over Karim and grabbed the sleeping Dominic.

"Come on, little fella. Time to rise and shine," she said, shooting Karim a questioning look.

Dominic, who'd inherited Karim's morning moodiness, frowned and tried to crawl to get under his father.

"Oh no you don't," Lisa said, grabbing her chubby little boy before he could get away. "You have to go to school, little buddy."

"Noooooo," Dominic said as he desperately tried to get away.

"Karim, I meant to tell you, Nadiah called while you were out. Sounded like something was wrong, but she didn't share with me," Lisa said, picking up the telephone and checking the caller ID. "It was around two-thirty."

"She must need something."

"Well, call her back," Lisa said, taking Dominic into the bathroom to wash him up. "She *is* your only sister."

"That she is," Karim said, still lying down, rubbing his head.

The doorbell rang.

"What the . . . ? Who is that at this time of morning?" Karim said, jumping up and stomping his way over the cold hardwood floors of their Stone Mountain townhouse. He cursed as he hustled down the stairs, through the foyer, and to the door. He peeped through the tiny glass and cursed again.

"Karim," the voice on the other side called. "I see you."

Karim took a deep breath and tried to calm himself.

It was Senior, the neighborhood nut case. The word was that Senior had taken some angel dust in his younger years and now, at forty, had the brain of an eight-year-old. All day, every day, he walked up and down the streets harassing people about doing odd jobs for them. He was harmless, but aggravating as a fly at barbecue.

"Senior, do you know what time it is? You out here ringing the damn doorbell like you took a laxative or something," Karim said.

"Sorry 'bout that, Dad," Senior said with his customary greeting for anyone born a male. "It's daylight, though."

"What does that have to do with anything?"

"Time to get up, Dad," Senior said with wide eyes. "Time to rise and shine, man."

"What are you, a rooster?"

"Come on, Dad, cut that out. Look here. I wanted to give you the first crack at these." Senior opened a plastic grocery bag filled with discarded television remotes.

"What?" Karim said, looking at his neighbor like he had finally flipped all the way out. "No thank you, man."

"Dad, you ain't even looked at 'em. I got Hitachi, Sony, Sharp, all the top brands, man."

"Senior, I want you to go home and take your medication."

"I'm good on that. Later for that. I gotta make money, Dad. Hustlas don't sleep." Senior smiled.

Karim's neck automatically jerked in for a closer look. *This dude has one tooth,* he noticed as he tried not to laugh. He was already missing about twenty-six of the thirty-two; now he seemed to have lost a few more.

"No thanks, Senior. I gotta go now," Karim said as he tried to close the door, but Senior put his foot in the jamb to stop him.

"Dad, wait up. I'll give 'em to you for the low low."

"Senior, I don't want those things for the no no. Now get your foot out of my door before I break it."

"You ain't gotta do me like that, Dad, but it's cool. Just let me hold two dollars until Friday."

"Today *is* Friday," Karim said.

"For real?" Senior asked. He slapped his pockets like he was looking for something. "Okay, Dad. I'll holla at you later, okay?"

"Okay, Senior." Karim shook his head as he pushed the door closed and locked it.

"Who was that?" Lisa asked as Karim walked back into the bedroom.

"Who do you think?"

She chuckled.

"Six-thirty in the morning and he's trying to sell some old remote controls."

"Remote controls," Lisa said, laughing as she returned from Dominic's room with his clothes.

"Man, that dude is tossed off in the head." Karim rubbed his own temples. "Did you know he only has one tooth?"

"I thought he had four."

"Somebody must've knocked the other three out. Now it's just that one hanging from the top of his mouth. Then he had the nerve to smile like he's on a dental plan. Oh . . . ," Karim said, lying across the bed on his stomach. "My head is about to explode."

"Well, I would suggest you go to the doctor, but that's just a hangover. Are you going to work?"

"I don't think so. I might pull the laptop out later, but I can't deal with that traffic this morning." Karim rolled over on his back.

"Karim," Lisa said. "Now, I don't want to be a nag and I know you're grown, but when you start taking off from work because you had too much to drink, don't you think that's a problem?"

"I don't have a problem, but I appreciate your concern."

Lisa stared at him without saying a word, then walked over and leaned down to give him a good-bye kiss.

"I can still smell the liquor on your breath. Go brush your teeth," she said, tossing their son's book bag over her shoulder.

"Look at this handsome fella," Karim said, sitting up and reaching his arms out for his son. "Who do you look like?"

"Daddddddyyyy," Dominic said, running into his father's outstretched arms.

Karim kissed him on his forehead, lips, and cheeks and hugged him tight. "Man, you're going to be the sharpest guy on the campus today."

"Hey, Daddy," Dominic said, rubbing his eyes. All of a sudden the little guy covered his nose. "Your breath stinks."

"Man, you just heard your mom say that. Stop being a follower."

"It does, Daddy," Dominic said, and he maneuvered his little body trying to get out of his father's arms.

"Oh, it's like that, huh?" Karim said, giving his son a slight shove. "Well, get on then. Ya little sellout. I thought you were my homey."

"Daddy, can you brush your teeth so you can take me to school?" Dominic asked.

Karim chuckled. "Mommy's gonna take you to school today, buddy. Daddy's not feeling well."

"You're not coughing," Dominic said, looking up with his big brown eyes.

"I don't have a cold. I got a headache."

"I wanna stay with you, Daddy," Dominic whined.

"Not today, my man. Your class is going on a field trip. Did you forget?"

"I don't wanna go," Dominic pouted. "I wanna stay with you."

Karim smiled but wanted to cry at the same time. He stared at Dominic's innocent face and a flash of his demons came into view. Karim forced himself back to the present.

Dominic walked over to his father and wiped away a tear that was making its way down Karim's cheek.

Lisa hustled back into the room fully dressed, with her briefcase in her hand.

" 'Bye, sweetie. I'll see you this afternoon," she said.

"Have a good day," Karim said, forcing a smile. "See ya later, li'l buddy."

" 'Bye, Daddy," Dominic said, staring into his father's eyes.

Karim stared back into his son's eyes. Something was special about this child. It was as if he knew his secret and was here to make everything okay again. Most little kids would ask why he was crying, but Dominic just stood there without a word. It was as if he was God's son masquerading around as a little boy.

"I'll take you to get some ice cream when you come home today. Okay?" Karim said.

"Okay," Dominic said with an instant smile.

Karim walked his family to the door and watched them until they were safe in the car and backing out of the driveway.

He walked back into his bedroom and looked at the clock. It was already eight o'clock.

He thought about going into his office, but just the thought made his head hurt even more. He would have to call in sick.

Karim crawled back into his bed and grabbed the telephone. He dialed his office number and started a fake cough. He put on his best sick voice.

"Mellon Financial Corporation. How may I help you?"

"Good morning, Maggie. This is Karim. I'm not feeling well so I'm going to stay in today. Coming down with a cold or something."

"Oh no," Maggie, the company's secretary, said. "Well, get you some vitamin C and some echinacea tea."

"Thanks. I'll try that."

"I'll pass the message along. Take care of yourself."

"I will, and I'll see you on Monday," Karim said, hanging up the phone and getting back out of the bed.

He walked into the bathroom and brushed his teeth. Once he was done with his other bathroom duties, he returned to his California king-sized bed and found a comfortable spot, intent on enjoying a peaceful Friday.

He grabbed the remote, pointed it at the plasma screen hanging over the fireplace on the far wall, and flipped channels until he found *Sports Center*.

Just as Karim had settled into a comfortable spot, the house phone rang. He looked at the caller ID and ignored it. It was Nadiah, and the call could only mean one of two things: either she wanted something or she needed something. Either way, it would have to wait.

Karim reached over and turned the ringer off. Less than a minute later, his cell phone rang. He looked at the small screen.

Same number. Same response.

He let the call go to his voice mail and pulled the covers over his shoulders.

A deep, sound sleep followed but he was jarred awake by the chimes of his doorbell.

Karim rolled over and stared at the ceiling. He couldn't believe this.

He jumped up and headed to the door, hell-bent on choking the life out of Senior. He looked through the glass, and what he saw was even worse than Senior.

"Damn," he said before opening the door.

2

Decatur, Georgia, was like any other place in the country. It had its good parts and bad parts. Some parts were simply breathtaking in their beauty, with high-priced homes and clean streets, but there were other parts that could take your breath away with their violence and poverty. The place Nadiah Spencer called home was one of the bad. Addicts of all sorts roamed the streets all times of day and night, seeking out their next high or plotting their next crime.

Nadiah thought she had seen the last of this place when she moved out six months ago to the good part of Decatur, but here she was back at home.

Starting over was a good thing. She needed a fresh start. She had finally learned that life offered no shortcuts and no man held the solution to her problems. It was a hard lesson to learn but after a few bad breaks, she was finally getting it.

This last one's name was Nick, and he was sweet as candy the first two months they dated but sour as grapes after that. This was her second go-around with Nick. She'd dated him six years ago, but he was a major cheater. For some strange reason she thought he had grown out of it, but for Nick, being a dog was a part of his DNA.

This time he'd graduated from cheating and wanted to start hitting.

Major mistake.

That was where she drew the line. Nadiah Spencer was nobody's punching bag.

Nick ranted and raved that he was going to kill her if she left him but the entire time he was screaming, she was packing. And now here she was, back home at Momma Mae's.

Nadiah looked around the small, stuffy room and thought about the good and the bad of the old days. Now she was back at the very same house she grew up in. The house had its share of fond and not-so-fond memories, but one thing was for sure: there was never a dull moment at 324 South Vain Street in Decatur, Georgia.

South Vain was a hard place to live. It was like party central, 24/7, but especially on Sundays.

Her grandmother, Mable "Mae" Harrison, sold liquor and beer out of a back room that was once a sun porch. The state of Georgia prohibited stores from selling alcohol on Sundays. So with the exception of fine restaurants and bars, Mae's illegal stock was the only option for the residents of Decatur who had an urge for the spirits. During the week she only doubled her prices after regular store hours but on Sundays, she tripled them. All times of day and night, people would knock on the back door to get their medicine at Mae's.

A can of Budweiser cost two dollars. A shot of cheap liquor was four dollars, and the ghetto folks of Decatur spent their last dime there because they weren't disciplined enough to bulk up on Saturday when they could get decent prices.

Nadiah walked past a few drunks arguing about some sporting event. An old lady sat in a chair in the kitchen, nodding her head to a drunken rhythm.

"Mrs. Jackson, you know if Momma catch you in here she's gonna put you out," Nadiah said, opening the refrigerator.

Mrs. Jackson lifted her head and showed off a tobacco-stained smile.

"Looks like you had a little too much to drink," Nadiah said.

"I'm 'bout to go. Just getting rested up a li'l bit. How you?"

"I'm doing okay. You doing okay?"

"Well I'm coming down with a . . ."

Nadiah walked out before Mrs. Jackson could finish. She hated being rude but if she wasn't, she'd be there for the rest of the morning listening to the ailments of the neighborhood hypochondriac.

Nadiah looked at the clock on the wall and saw that it was almost four in the morning. She grabbed her laptop computer and headed out to the front porch where it was quiet.

Nadiah always enjoyed the wee hours of the morning. Even though behind the walls of the house chaos was at its peak, out on the front porch she was at peace.

She pulled out her Philly blunt and lit it. She had always

enjoyed the earth's essence more than she cared to admit, but it made her feel good. And that was all she was looking for right now. Life was a struggle, and her marijuana kept her sane. She placed the blunt to her lips and took a puff. She thought of the old Jimi Hendrix tune "Purple Haze" as the smoke invaded her senses.

She closed her eyes and thought about how she would write the next scene in her novel. She had been working on the book for the last three years and it was finally coming together. As a matter of fact, she was looking to wrap the story up any day now.

MOMMA'S A VIRGIN: A NOVEL
by Nadiah Spencer

She could see it now. A smile creased her face as she visualized sitting behind a table at Barnes & Noble at Rockefeller Center in New York as people lined up to get their books signed.

Oprah, please call me, she whispered to herself.

Nadiah opened up the laptop and waited for the antiquated box to boot up. She took another puff of the haze and moaned. Once the computer was ready, she attacked her book with a passion. Her fingers raced across the keyboard.

She had a story to tell and she was hell-bent on telling it. The story was about a woman who had two kids but had never willingly given herself to a man. She was molested as a child, raped as an adult, and coerced into sex by conniving baby daddies. That was until she met a man who changed her entire world. And for the first time in her life, she wanted to share herself with a man.

It was her story, but she was having trouble with the ending because in real life, she had yet to meet that man.

Writing was therapeutic; it soothed her soul. When she was writing she felt no pain and her life wasn't out of whack.

Just as she got into a really emotional chapter, her cell phone rang.

It was Nick.

She looked at the phone for a long time. It rang four times before she finally hit the end button to send it to voice mail. She already missed living with him. He was fine as hell and could make her legs shake with his tongue skills, but she was done with him because he'd been stupid enough to put his hands on her.

She pressed the menu button and went into her address book to edit his name. His new name was DON'T ANSWER. She hit "save" and started scrolling through other numbers. After she was done, Nadiah had edited thirty-two names—all of them men—and every last one of them had DON'T AN-SWER as his new moniker.

Nadiah found herself getting aggravated at the thought of some of the things she had allowed to happen in her life. She puffed the haze again and held it in until she started coughing. She exhaled and rested her head on the back of the chair. As the weed took its effect, calmness washed over her and she slowly let life's issues go. She could feel her baggage drifting from her body and into the wind of the cool November breeze.

She was done with all the things that had been bringing

her down. That's why she never told anyone about her book, because the ghetto was full of negative energy, and she wasn't going to have her dreams shattered by someone else's pessimistic view on life.

"Damn, this fool done took me outta my zone," she said as she reread the last sentence she had written.

The house phone rang, and Nadiah frowned as she looked at the caller ID.

"Out of Area," it read.

She let the call go to voice mail, but just as soon as it stopped ringing, it started again.

"If this is another one of those fast-ass little girls calling for my son, I'mma flip my wig." She answered the phone. "Hello?"

"You have a call from an inmate at the DeKalb County Jail," an electronic voice said. "Caller, state your name."

"JaQuan," the voice said.

Nadiah almost dropped her laptop as she jumped to her feet. At the last second she reached out and grabbed it.

"Press the number one to accept," the electronic voice said.

She pushed the number one as she stormed into the house, making a beeline for her son's room.

"Ma," JaQuan said.

Nadiah looked at the empty bed and the open window.

"What," she growled, "in the hell are you doing in jail?"

"It wasn't even my fault. These fools think I'mma pimp."

"What?" Nadiah almost screamed.

"Yeah, they jumped out and locked me up for nuttin'. Can you come and get me?"

Nadiah closed her eyes and exhaled.

From day one she had been both mother and father to
JaQuan. His sorry sperm donor bailed out right after the con-
dom broke and never surfaced again. Nadia knew she wasn't
going to be getting any awards for mother of the year, but she
did the best she could for him, and all she got for her efforts
was a truant hell-bent on ruining his life.

"What are you doing out of the house in the first place?"

"It was too loud to sleep so I just went out for a walk. Ain't
no crime in that. How they gonna lock me up and call me a
pimp?"

"I guess I look like a fool, huh?" Nadiah said. "You think
you can tell me anything, don't you?"

"Come on, Ma, it stinks in here," JaQuan said, sounding
like the fifteen-year-old he was.

"Well, good. Take a deep breath, because that's where your
little ass will be staying."

"Ma, don't do me like that!"

Nadiah couldn't stop her heart from racing. She wanted to
mean the words she said, but she knew she didn't. Outside of
a paramedic calling to say her son was killed, this was the one
call she most dreaded.

People who came up like she did looked at jail as a rite of
passage into manhood. Like going to jail was the thing to do.
There was no shame in it in the 'hood. But she'd never wanted
that for JaQuan. She'd worked the day shift and the late-night
shift just to put him in a private elementary school because the
public schools in their neighborhood were more like breeding
grounds for Georgia's future criminals. The teachers weren't
interested in teaching and the principal was so incompetent
you'd think he was born a Bush.

"They say you can bail me out," JaQuan whined.

"Why would I do that?"

"Come on, Ma," JaQuan pleaded, sounding like he was crying.

"You know what? That's what you get for trying to be slick. Why don't you think, JaQuan? Anything could've happened to you being out there this time of morning."

"I know. But I swear I just went for a walk."

"JaQuan, you know I need my money to get that car fixed. Why don't you think? 'Bye."

"Ma," JaQuan called.

"What?"

"I love you," he said.

"Oh, *now* you love me? You won't say two words to me any other time. But now you need me and you wanna pull out the love word."

JaQuan didn't respond.

" 'Bye," Nadiah said again, hanging up the phone.

She closed her laptop. She was really out of her zone now, and her high was completely blown. There would be no more writing this morning.

Nadia walked into the house and went straight to the back room, where Momma Mae was sitting at a card table playing a hand of bid whist.

"Momma, can I talk to you for a minute?"

"Whatchu want?" Momma Mae said, studying her cards.

Sitting on the table in front of her was what she called her "peacemaker," a long silver gun that was almost as tall as she was. On occasion, when things got a little too rowdy at her place, Momma Mae would reach out and touch her peacemaker. *Now you can make peace up in here or meet your maker, but one way or another I'm gonna have my peace,* she would say before cocking back the hammer.

"I need to talk to you," Nadiah said.

"If it has anything to do with money, the answer is no," Momma Mae said, tossing a card on the table. "You already owe me two hundred dollars."

The derelicts around the table laughed.

Nadiah wasn't in the mood.

"I'll loan you a little something," a man from across the room said with a lustful look on his face.

Momma Mae shot the man a quick stare. "Time for you to leave," she said to the man without raising her voice.

"Come on, Mae, I was just fooling with the girl," the man said, fanning her off.

Momma Mae placed her cards on the table and reached for the peacemaker.

The man got the message and eased on out the back door.

Her word was the law, and once she said something there was no more discussing it.

"JaQuan is locked up," Nadiah said.

"For what?" Momma Mae said calmly, as if her great-grandchild being incarcerated was nothing out of the ordinary.

Nadiah looked at her grandmother but couldn't find any words.

Momma Mae raised her eyebrows and gave Nadiah a look of pity and contempt. When Nadiah didn't say anything, she went back to playing cards.

Nadiah went into her bedroom and dialed her brother's number.

"Hello," a sleepy female voice answered.

"Lisa. Is Karim there?"

"No, he went out, but . . . what time is it?"

"A little after four."

"He should be back shortly. Is everything okay?"

"No," Nadiah said. "Can you tell him to call me the minute he gets in?"

"Okay. Is there anything I can do?"

"No. Just tell Karim to call me."

"Okay."

Nadiah hung up the phone and sat on the side of her bed. She thought about her son sitting in a stinking jail cell and closed her eyes to stop the tears.

3

"What's up?" Karim said, standing in the doorway wearing a pair of boxer briefs, not bothering to invite his guest in.

"Why you not answering your phone?"

"Well come on in," Karim said sarcastically as his sister barged in past him without waiting on an invite.

"Put on some clothes," she said.

"Last I checked I was home."

"What are you doing home? Your job said you were out sick. You don't look sick to me," Nadiah said, eyeing him up and down. "Did you get fired?"

"What do you want, girl?" Karim snapped, already irritated.

"Damn you evil," she said, looking around. "Lisa got this joint looking nice. Tell her bougie ass I said do the damn thing."

"Nadiah," Karim said, still holding the door open. "I know you didn't come over here to talk about decorating. Spit it out. I'm tired and I'm trynna get back to bed."

Nadiah looked at her brother, then cast her eyes downward. Karim could see that something was really bothering her.

"That ignorant-ass little boy I have for a son done got himself locked up. I'm flat broke, so I was trying to see if you could help me out."

"No," Karim said flatly.

"Why?"

"Because I don't want to," Karim said.

"So you just gonna leave your nephew in jail like that?"

"I didn't take him to jail. So how could I leave him there?"

"You know what I mean, Karim," Nadia pleaded. "Please."

"No."

"I'll pay you back. I mean if I had the money, I wouldn't even be here."

Karim didn't answer. He finally closed the door behind him.

"What is he locked up for?" he asked, walking into the kitchen, then into the pantry. "You hungry?"

"No."

Karim returned from the pantry with one of his son's morning breakfast bars. "So what is he locked up for?"

Nadiah lowered her eyes again. Karim couldn't tell if it was shame or guilt. Maybe both.

"Pimping," she said in a breath just above a whisper.

"*Pimping?* JaQuan's fifteen," Karim almost screamed. "Who in the hell is he pimping?"

"I can't tell that boy nothing. He snuck out of the house. I can't keep an eye on him 24/7."

"Of course you can't. You can't seem to do anything that real parents find ways to do. How many times did he fail the first grade? Who in the hell fails the first damn grade? You couldn't find the time to teach the boy his ABC's, but he knew every damn rap song on the radio. Then you wanna blame the schools. Spent all that money on private schools like that was gonna solve the problem when all along the problem was you. So, hell no, you can't tell him nothing. They should let him out and lock *your* ass up," Karim said.

Nadiah looked up into her brother's eyes but didn't say anything.

Karim held her gaze. He couldn't tell if she really cared or was just doing what she thought she should do.

All of a sudden Nadiah turned away. Her focus was now on a painting on the wall.

"Nadiah?" Karim said.

She ignored him and kept looking at the painting as if she were in a gallery.

"Nadiah," he said a little louder.

"What?"

"Did you hear me?"

"I heard you."

"I mean, come on. What did you expect? Do you remember when we were there for Thanksgiving dinner and you were calling him a pimp? You don't find that ironic that he's out there trying to live up to your lofty expectations?"

"I was just joking, man. It was a figure of speech. I wasn't telling him to go out there and be no damn pimp," Nadiah said. "Get real."

"*You* get real. You might as well have told him to take his little narrow behind out there and be one."

"So you're an angel?" Nadiah said with a knowing look on her face. "If my memory is still in full effect, I would think not."

Karim's heart stopped.

With the exception of his brother Omar, Nadiah was the only person who knew what haunted him. He couldn't believe she was trying to use that information to her benefit right now.

Karim gritted his teeth and looked away. It took only a few seconds for him to gather himself.

"What happened to your neck?" he asked, looking at the white gauze taped to his sister's neck. He needed to change the subject.

"Tattoo," Nadiah said calmly, as if there was nothing out of the ordinary about having a tattoo on your neck.

"I guess you don't really want a job, hunh?"

"I got a job."

"Being a stripper isn't exactly a long-term plan. Don't think they have 401k's for y'all, do they?"

"That's my business, Karim. If you're so concerned about what I do, then you get me a job doing something else."

"Whatever, Nadiah," Karim said. "You're already beige. How do you think you can hide a tattoo on your neck?"

"I ain't trynna hide it."

Karim's lip couldn't curl any further into a snarl.

"Don't stand there and judge me. I am who I am. Who-ever don't like it, can keep it moving," Nadiah said, rolling her neck.

"So you're good. Everyone in this world should change and conform to your standards, or should I say lack of stan-dards?"

"I don't give a damn what everyone else does. I'm Nadiah Spencer and that's the only person I'm concerned about pleas-ing."

"And that's the mentality that has JaQuan Spencer locked up."

That got Nadiah's attention. She shot Karim a look that said his words had hit her below the belt.

Karim fanned her off.

"You need to get it together, little girl," he said. "Just be-cause you can have sex doesn't mean you can be a good par-ent."

"I am a good mom."

"Buying Jordans and PlayStation games doesn't qualify. Anybody can do that. When is the last time you sat down and checked JaQuan's homework?" Karim snapped. "Where is he?"

Nadiah huffed, as if she didn't appreciate the dressing-down.

"Where is he?"

"DeKalb County," she said.

"What is he doing in DeKalb County? I thought you lived in Fulton."

"I'm back at home now."

"Why?"

"Because I was living with a fool and I didn't want to catch a murder case. That's why."

Karim shook his head. It was always something with her. "Give me a second. Let me get dressed."

4

Nadiah browsed around the lower level of Karim's house while she waited for him to get dressed.

She couldn't help but admire how comfortable Karim's life seemed to be. Looking at all of the material possessions, she felt a twinge of envy. He had flat-panel televisions, leather furniture, hardwood floors, and some of the most amazing artwork. She couldn't help but compare what he had to what she didn't have. They'd been raised together, been through more than their share of drama together, yet he seemed to rise above it all and was living the life, while she dwelled in relative hell.

Nadiah found her way over to a particular painting and stared long and hard at it. She was studying the artist's style. She dug into the hues he used, the strokes and the texture, and found herself becoming angry. The piece was okay, but she was way better than this guy, and here he was prominently displayed on her brother's wall.

Karim had never asked her to do a picture for him and he was the main one encouraging her to paint. If he would only invest in her, both of them would benefit greatly. But she could never ask him to do that and he never offered.

Nadiah forced herself away from the canvases and walked into the kitchen. She was stopped dead in her tracks by an awesome view of Stone Mountain. She could actually see the faces etched into the stone on the side of the mountain.

On the counter by the window was a framed picture of her nephew Dominic. He was dressed in a cute little white shirt with a bow tie. He had the prettiest smile, and it brightened her mood. Even though Karim did a damn good job of keeping the little fella away from her, just looking at him made her feel good inside. She picked the photo up and slid it in her pocket, frame and all.

She thought about what she had just done, and wondered why she didn't feel comfortable enough with her brother to ask for a picture of her own nephew.

Was she that bad?

No.

Karim is just an asshole, she thought.

"How did you get here?" Karim asked as he walked into the kitchen and motioned for her to follow him down into the garage.

"Maceo," Nadiah said, still seething inside. She took one last look around and followed her brother outside.

Karim hit a button on the wall and the garage door rose. Nadiah walked to the passenger door and he walked around to the driver's side of his Ford Explorer.

"Maceo. What's he up to?" Karim said once he was strapped in.

"Same old thing. Getting his hustle on. He's doing good, though."

Maceo was a neighborhood kid Karim grew up with. He was one of the most gifted athletes to ever touch a ball filled with air, but his lack of guidance and poor choices had led him to toss all of his athletic gifts away and settle for the life of a street hustler.

"Still selling drugs?"

"Yep."

"Then how is he doing good?"

"Because, he is," Nadiah snapped.

"Man, that has to the biggest waste of potential I've ever seen. He could've gotten his money the legitimate way," Karim said, backing out of his driveway. "Put your seat belt on."

Nadiah looked at her brother with a strange and confused expression on her face. She didn't get him.

"What?" Karim asked, trying to read her.

"Why are you always judging people?"

"I'm not judging anybody. I'm just stating the facts. That boy had hundreds of scholarships coming out of high school and he decides to stay home and hustle. That's not a judgment, that's a fact, and if you ask me, a plain stupid one."

"It's a good thing nobody asked you. Just because he didn't go to college and learn a bunch of B.S. he's stupid?"

"Pretty much." Karim hunched his shoulder and maneuvered around Senior, who was standing in the middle of the street trying to flag him down.

Nadiah shook her head in disgust.

"Look how you treat people!" Nadiah looked back at Senior. "That man wasn't up to your standards so you couldn't stop to see what he wanted? You've changed, Karim."

"First of all, you shouldn't assume things. Second of all, I didn't change, I matured," Karim said, turning out onto the highway headed toward Momma Mae's house off Glenwood Road in Decatur.

"I'm just saying, it's like you forgot where you came from."

"I haven't forgotten. Just because I don't run around bragging and acting all ignorant doesn't mean I forgot where I came from. But I'm not throwing up the East Side like it's something to be proud of." Karim did some funky little twist with his fingers and made a dumb-looking face.

"It ain't nothing to be ashamed of, either. That's who you are. Don't be ashamed of who you are," Nadiah said.

"I'm not ashamed of it and it's not *who* I am. It's where I'm from. There is a difference."

"So why aren't you proud of where you're from?"

"What is there to be proud of? I mean it is what it is, but living with roaches, being broke and hungry all the time is nothing to be proud of. Crackheads, hookers, and a bunch of underachievers all over the place. Come on, man. Don't be ridiculous."

"I'm just saying. You got a little job and now you look down on the people you came up with."

"I don't look down on anybody," Karim defended. "Look, you do whatever you feel, just don't expect me to be singing your praises for dumb shit."

"Oh, it's dumb because the great Karim said so, hunh?"

"Whatever. The Bible says don't cast your pearls to swine. So I'm shutting up with your ignorant ass."

"Fuck you, Karim," Nadiah spat.

"Fuck you, too," Karim spat back.

Nadiah turned her head and stared out the window.

They pulled into the driveway of the house on South Vain Street.

"Come on in if you don't mind breathing a little ghetto air," Nadiah said sarcastically.

Karim put his vehicle in park and stepped out. He locked the doors and when he turned around, Monroe, one of the many drunks who lived nearby, was standing in his face.

"Boo," Monroe said with bloodshot eyes that threatened to pop out of his head.

Karim jumped back.

"Nadiah, give me a hug?" Monroe said.

"Wait on it," Nadiah said, walking away.

"Monroe, you trynna get knocked out?" Karim said.

"Look at him, Nadiah. Still trynna be big brah," Monroe said.

"Monroe, go home," Nadiah said over her shoulder. "You know Momma don't like you around here begging."

"I ain't begging. I had a vision. I saw Karim reaching in his pockets and taking care of my itchy palms. Let me hold something, K-man. Anything. Everything. Just let me hold something," Monroe said, rubbing his hard hands together.

"You keep on rubbing those crusty things together like that and you're gonna start a fire," Karim said, reaching into his pockets and pulling out two dollars for Monroe.

"Damn, you a'ight with me, boy. How's life at the big-time suit-wearing tall buildings?"

"All is well," Karim said.

"Good Lawd," Monroe said, looking at Nadiah as her shapely rear end switched from side to side up the driveway.

"Monroe," Karim snapped. "If you don't get your old perverted eyes off of my sister's butt, I'mma have to do something to you."

Monroe jumped back into a fighter's stance. "You hit me I'll sue you," he said with an ugly chuckle.

Nadiah walked into her house and left the door open for Karim. Then she went to her bedroom.

Karim walked in and went straight over to his seventy-three-year-old grandmother. He leaned down to give her a peck on the cheek.

"Good morning, good-looking," Karim said.

"Hey baby." Momma Mae smiled proudly at her grandson.

"Momma, who been in my room?" Nadiah asked, rushing back out into the living room.

"I didn't know you had a room," Momma Mae said. "Last I checked, all of 'em were mine."

"Momma," Nadiah whined. "Somebody's been in my drawers!"

"Ain't nobody been in that room, girl. You be smoking that stuff so much you probably forgot you left it open."

"I don't be that high. You always giving something the remix," Nadiah said.

"I bet I'll get out of this chair and remix your little high-yellow ass," Momma Mae said.

Nadiah looked at Karim and they shared a laugh at their fiery grandmother's expense. Their spat was over just as soon as it had started.

Momma Mae raised Karim, Nadiah, and Omar, their older brother, from the time they were little kids after their mother passed away. Their father was buried with a closed casket after a bullet disfigured his face.

Nadiah went back into her bedroom and tossed clothes out of her way as she walked around the room, looking for the last purse she had used.

"What are you looking for?" Momma Mae asked.

"My ID," Nadiah said from the bedroom. "I'mma raise some hell if I don't find my purse."

"Seems to me that's all you do is raise hell."

"Don't start with me, Momma. I ain't in the mood," Nadiah snapped.

"Ask me if I give a hoot about your moods. I bet I'll knock yo' head off, you keep getting sassy with me."

"I got it," Nadiah said, walking out of the room with her purse.

"Where you going looking like that?"

"I'm going to get JaQuan."

"You go down to that jail looking like that and they gonna think the boy is guilty, 'cause you sure look like you one of his hoes coming to bail him out," Momma Mae said, frowning at the skin-tight jeans and body-hugging shirt that might as well have been a bra. "If I was a man looking at you, the only thing on my mind would be something nasty."

"Whatever," Nadiah said. She thought she looked nice.

"I already told you about dressing like that. I damn near had to kill a fool last night over your hoochie-dressing self."

"Momma, please leave me alone," Nadiah pleaded. She wasn't in the mood for her grandmother's old-school bashing.

"Please nothing. You got everything mixed up, chile. Yeah, you can get a man dressed like that. Well, not no real man, 'cause a real man don't want his woman dressed like some streetwalker. Karim," Momma Mae called.

"Yes, Ma'am," Karim said with a chuckle.

"She had a date last week and the sorry bastard wouldn't even get out of the car to come to the door. Just blew the horn. I guess she got drive-through coochie," Momma Mae cackled.

Karim laughed and shook his head.

"Whatever, Momma," Nadiah said. "Nobody got no time to be ringing no doorbell with flowers behind their back. That wasn't no date anyway. That was Nick."

"Oh, now you tell me. I wish I would've known it was him; I'd be locked up right now myself. Did your sister tell you she moved back home because that fool went upside her head?" Momma Mae said to Karim.

Karim's eyes shot toward Nadiah. She looked away.

"But that's what she gets," Momma Mae continued. "Every time I look up she living with a different man. And not nare one of 'em thought enough of her to change her last name."

"Maybe I didn't want their last names."

"But you wanted to lay up with 'em."

Nadiah waved her off and put on her coat. "You ready, Karim? I ain't trying to sit here and listen to all this mess."

"You need to listen." The small and fragile woman moved with surprising swiftness as she jumped into Nadiah's face. "Your life is a damn mess. It's your fault that baby is in jail in the first place."

"How is it my fault?" Nadiah snapped back. "I didn't tell his dumb ass to sneak outta the house and go try to pimp some damn body."

"You cuss one mo' time under my roof," Momma Mae threatened.

Nadiah rolled her eyes.

"Now, it's your fault 'cause you unfit. Where ya daughter at? 'Course, though, I don't blame her daddy one bit for taking her from you. Next thing you know, the chile would've been 'round here dressing like you."

Nadiah glared at Momma Mae. *Why did she have to go there?* she wondered.

"You get on my nerves, girl," Momma Mae said.

"You get on mine," Nadiah shot back.

"You free to leave."

"So are you. Granddaddy left my name on the house just like yours. So *you* leave."

"I bet if I put a hole in your ass you name won't be on there no more," Momma Mae said with a straight face. It was the funniest thing in the world.

Nadiah started laughing and shook her head. She looked at Karim, and he seemed to be on the verge of tears. He was standing by the fireplace, staring at a picture that needed to be removed.

"Karim, let's go," Nadiah said, watching her brother closely.

Karim put the picture back and walked over to give his grandmother a hug.

"Bring your baby over here sometime," Momma Mae said.

"I will," he said before walking out.

"You always say that. You need to let him spend some time with his granny," Momma Mae said to Karim's back.

"The last time I brought him over here you gave him some liquor," Karim said, still walking.

"That's 'cause he had a cold. A little nip won't hurt him," Momma Mae said.

5

The ride to the DeKalb County Detention Center was a quiet one. Karim didn't feel like talking, because his mind was in a bad place. Seeing that picture at Momma Mae's brought back so many horrible memories.

Karim stole glances at Nadiah. Her eyes were closed, but her rest wasn't peaceful. She was a woman whose life was in constant turmoil. She frowned at the thoughts wreaking chaos in her head. Sucked her teeth at the demons and grunted away memories of pain. At least that's how he saw it.

"This the first and last time I'm doing this," Nadiah said out of the blue.

Karim looked at her. She was staring in front of her with a dead look in her eyes.

"Yeah, it is," Nadiah said turning to him. "And you can save the sermon. Preacher."

"First of all, I didn't say anything. Second of all, why do you think someone is preaching when they tell you about yourself?" Karim said as he whipped his truck into the parking lot.

"And who are you to tell me about myself? Please tell me who died and made you chief?"

Karim wasn't trying to get into it again with her. He put the truck in park and jumped out.

"Damn," Nadiah said, staring up at the ten-story building. "I never thought . . . ," she said but stopped herself.

Karim frowned at her. She was getting on his nerves with her denial and for being stuck on stupid. For the life of him, he couldn't see why she hadn't seen this one coming.

They walked up to the entrance of the jail and Karim held the door for his sister. Once inside the lobby, they headed straight for the sign that read "Duty Officer."

"How may I help you?" a chubby-cheeked desk sergeant said, never looking up from his sandwich.

"I'm here to pick up my son, JaQuan Spencer," Nadiah said.

"Fill out this form and have a seat over there."

Nadiah filled out the papers and took a seat.

Karim didn't say anything, and once again they ignored each other. Karim was reading a newspaper that someone had left on the table, and Nadiah busied herself by filing her nails.

"Nadiah Spencer," the desk sergeant called after nearly an hour. "Your son is not here."

"Whatchu mean he's not here? He called me from here. Where is he?"

"Calm down. He's a juvenile, so he's over off of Panthersville Road. We just process 'em over here, then we ship the youngins over there to the youth facility."

"Where is that?"

"I know where it is," Karim said. He had visited the kiddie jail on a few different occasions during his brief stint working for the state prosecutor's office.

"But we need five hundred dollars before I can release him to you," the desk sergeant said.

"This is his first offense. Why y'all trynna break people?"

"I don't make the laws, ma'am, I just enforce them." The guard looked at JaQuan's paperwork and smiled. "So he wants to be a pimp, huh?"

"That's what y'all saying. You only know what you read, so you can shut the hell up," Nadiah blasted the man.

"Excuse me?" the guard said, his chubby cheeks turning tomato red.

"You heard me. Don't nobody pay you for your opinion," she said before walking back to the seating area.

Karim walked over to the cash machine in the corner of the lobby. He wanted to scream as he punched in his PIN. It was so hard for him to throw money away, and that was exactly what he was doing. Things were already tight for him, and now he was digging his hole a little deeper. He couldn't believe he was doing this, but nevertheless he got the money and walked back to the desk to hand over his hard-earned cash.

The sergeant, still red as a beet, pushed a clipboard in front of Karim.

"Sign right here," he said.

"Do you need his mother to sign, or . . ."

"I don't care," Chubby Cheeks said.

Karim hunched his shoulders and signed the papers. He took the paperwork that was handed to him and headed out of the lobby. "Let's go," he said to his sister.

Ten minutes later they were pulling into the parking lot of a small building that looked more like a factory than a jail.

They got out of the truck and walked the short distance up to the front of the building. That's when the place started to look like a jail. A stainless-steel call box was mounted on the wall by the front entrance.

Karim pressed the button.

"How may I help you?" a voice squawked.

"We're here to pick up JaQuan Spencer."

"Do you have any weapons, knives, or any other contraband that you see listed on the wall in front of you?" the same voice said.

"No."

There was a loud and hard click as the locks of the steel doors disengaged. Karim and Nadiah walked through two more steel doors that made the same deafening clicks before they reached the lobby.

Two muscular guards, both well over six feet tall and wearing black army fatigues, stood by the doors of a cell in the lobby. Karim looked behind one of the guards and into the glass window of the cell and did a double take. The sight of his kin chained to a wall broke his heart. He felt his knees getting weak. Their eyes met, and Karim had to turn away.

"Why y'all got him like that?" Karim asked softly.

"He threatened to kill a staff member. We knew he was just running off at the mouth, so instead of bringing him up on more charges we just sent him to cool down."

"And that's how you cool him down?" Karim asked.

The guard hunched his shoulders. "I don't really agree with it, but I'm just here to follow orders. He seems to be a good kid, just acting out in front of the others. We didn't want to make a big deal out of it."

"Yeah, y'all sure are treating him like he's a good kid. Let my son outta that shit," Nadiah barked. "He ain't no goddamn Kunta Kente."

The guards ignored her and went on with their duties as if she'd never said a thing. Obviously this was not their first time facing an angry mother.

"You need to fill out that form right there so I can give you back his personal belongings," the guard at the desk said to Karim.

"I need to see the warden," Nadiah said.

"We don't have a warden," the guard said. "We have a director."

"Well, get the director then. This don't make no damn sense how y'all treating these kids. How y'all expect them to act if you treat 'em like that? I wouldn't chain a dog up like that. Now go get me the director right now," Nadiah screamed.

"We're okay," Karim said, overriding his sister.

"Oh no the hell we ain't." Nadiah turned on Karim. "That's my son, and I wanna see the damn warden."

"Ma'am, listen to me," the guard said. "If you want to see a supervisor then I'll get you one, but trust me, we're doing him a favor. Like I said, I don't think he belongs here because he's a good kid but if a supervisor comes here and looks up his infraction, he's going to write him up. If that happens he won't be going home today because they will take him right back down to the County jail and re-arrest him for assault on staff or simple battery. Now what he did wasn't that serious to me, but it's your call."

Nadiah huffed and wiped away the tears that were streaming down her face. She turned and looked at her son, and the floodgates came open.

"Everything's gonna be okay," Karim said. In a rare show of compassion, he pulled his sister close and gave her a hug. "Don't even sweat it."

The cell door popped open, and one of the guards went in and returned with JaQuan. His hair was some form of wild-looking dreadlocks mixed with naps. His dark skin glistened with sweat as he nodded at his uncle.

"Thank you for coming so quick, Ma," JaQuan said sarcastically.

"You better shut your damn mouth," Nadiah said. "You lucky I came at all."

JaQuan fanned her off and turned to his uncle. "What up, Unk?" he said as if he were being picked up from school rather than jail.

Karim nodded but was struck by his nonchalance.

"I need to get my clothes, man," JaQuan said to one of the

guards. "And I already heard about how y'all be stealing people's clothes, so don't even go there with me."

"Shut the hell up," Nadiah screamed as she slapped JaQuan so hard it sounded like a gun went off. "Who in the hell do you think you are?"

JaQuan held his face and frowned.

"Unk, you better get her," JaQuan said in a warning tone.

"Or what?" Nadiah said, rearing back for another slap before Karim grabbed her. "Your ass was about to cry on the phone, now you wanna act like you some thug who's use to this shit. Leave his ass in here, Karim."

"Nadiah, go and wait outside," Karim said, shielding his nephew from his mother's wrath.

"Nah hell, no," Nadiah said, going after her son again.

"Nadiah," Karim barked. He rarely ever raised his voice, and that got her attention.

One of the guards walked over. "Ma'am, I cannot let you assault your son in this center. So listen to my man right here. Go on and wait in the car and once we get him his personal property he'll be right out."

Nadiah clenched her fist and wiped away the new stream of tears flowing down her cheeks. She gave her son one last menacing stare, then barreled toward the door they'd entered and pushed. The door didn't budge. A loud click sounded and she was gone.

"Did ya tell my uncle 'bout how y'all did me?" JaQuan said, staring at one of the guards. "Yeah, fuck with somebody ya own size."

"Shut up, JaQuan," Karim said.

"Nah, Unk, these dudes ain't nuttin' but bullies. Punch my uncle in his damn chest and watch him mop the floor with yo' punk ass," JaQuan said to the only guard who hadn't spoken yet.

"I said shut up," Karim said.

"Come with me, Spencer," the guard who did all of the talking said as he walked into a room off the lobby.

A few minutes later, JaQuan walked out wearing his own clothes.

"Have a seat over there while I get your other items," the guard said.

JaQuan walked over to the guard who'd hit him.

"This ain't over," JaQuan said.

"Get the fuck outta my face, li'l nigga," the guard growled.

"I ain't scared of you, bitch," JaQuan said, not backing down.

"You need to be," the guard said.

"Well I ain't," JaQuan snapped. "Damn loser."

"You the one locked up," the guard said. "So who the loser?"

"Yo' big dumb ass make three dollars an hour."

"You 'bout to get fu . . ."

"Hey," Karim said to the guard. "So you gonna stoop down to a child's level?"

"You better get him before I teach him a lesson," the guard said.

"You're not here to teach lessons. You're not a judge nor are you a jury. If you think it makes you look tough because you can beat up on a kid then you need help."

"Man, you better get out of my face," the guard roared.

Karim didn't budge.

The guard must have seen something that he didn't like in Karim's eyes, because after one look at him he backed down.

Karim turned away from the guard and walked back over to the desk. The other guard handed him a brown bag, and JaQuan jumped up and grabbed it. He inspected the contents and paused.

"Where my grill at, cuz'?" JaQuan asked.

"Wherever it is, it needs to stay there," Karim said. "Come on."

"Nah, Unk, I paid a nice little grip for that," JaQuan said, not moving.

"You either come with me or take your chances in here."

JaQuan took a deep breath and gave his enemy one last menacing mug before following his uncle out of the kiddie jail.

"Man, that place ain't 'bout nothing," JaQuan said once they were outside. "Dudes up in there a joke."

"So is that the kind of life you're trying to live?" Karim asked.

"Nah, I'm just saying."

"Why are you out there pimping somebody?"

"Man, that wasn't nuttin' but a setup. Those shady cops just wanted to lock somebody up. It's all about the money, Unk," JaQuan said, smiling as if he were imparting some deep information.

"JaQuan," Karim said, placing both hands on his nephew's shoulders. "You're right this is a setup. That place isn't bad at all. It's meant to be that way, so you don't mind coming back. Slowly but surely you're institutionalized. Then when you hit the prisons, they got something for ya. You'll realize then that you've been played. Look at you. Smiling like it's all good. It's not, and you better wake up before it's too late. This isn't a joke, JaQuan. Nobody's playing games with you. Now you're gonna have to go to court for this and there is a possibility that you might get some time."

"This ain't nothing but my first offense. They can't give me no time for that bull . . . for that stuff. If anything, I'll get boot camp and all they do is yell and make you do push-ups. I went through that at football camp," JaQuan said with a smile.

"Get in the truck, man," Karim said, shaking his head.

"Karim," Nadiah said once Karim had closed his door and placed the key in the ignition.

"What's up?"

"I can't do nothing with him," she said, shaking her head from side to side with a look of defeat on her face. Her eyes looked as if someone had poured sand in them.

"You should've left him in there for a few days," Karim said.

"Maybe you can do something with him?" Nadiah asked hesitantly.

Karim looked into the rearview mirror and saw his nephew bobbing his head to his iPod. He turned and looked into his sister's teary eyes.

"When he was five years old and cussing you out, I asked you . . . no, I begged you to let me take him. But he was your baby and he was cute. Well, look what cute got you. Now you want help when he's fifteen years old and buck wild. I have a kid of my own and I'm not about to let him get influenced by that mess you created. You deal with it," Karim said, pulling out of the jail's parking lot.

6

Karim's office building was located in the trendy Atlantic Station area of Atlanta. He pulled into the towered parking deck and stepped out of his truck.

"Happy Monday morning, handsome," Mariah, a new staff attorney who worked at his building in a big-time law firm, said, walking up behind him.

"Hey," Karim said, turning around to greet the woman he and his co-workers lusted over daily as she strutted through the lobby during lunch hour in her high heels and short skirts. "How are ya?"

"Very well, now that I see that you're okay. I missed you on Friday," Mariah said.

"Is that right?"

"I heard you were sick. Are you feeling better?"

"I might make it." Karim smiled. "How did you know I was sick?"

She smiled.

"You're investigating me, counselor?"

"A little. Nah, I needed a lunch date, so I called your office looking for you."

"I see. Well, that was my loss."

"So are you feeling better now?"

"Yeah. Thanks for asking."

"I'm sure your wife took good care of you," Mariah said with a sly look on her face.

"I'm not married," Karim said. "But I'm involved," he added.

"So am I, but . . . ," Mariah said, rolling her eyes.

That little gesture let Karim know that she wasn't too happy at home.

They walked into the building and took the elevator to the sixth floor.

"Hopefully we can reschedule that lunch one day this week," Mariah said before the elevator stopped on her floor.

"Sounds good," Karim said.

"I'll send you an e-mail and we'll see if we can't get our dates to match up. Cool?"

"You got it," Karim said, watching her sexy legs as she stepped off the elevator.

Damn, that skirt is a problem, he thought, shaking his head.

The elevator closed and opened two flights up. He forced the thoughts of one of the finest women he'd ever seen from his head.

———

Mellon Financial Corporation was written in stainless steel letters over the large glass doors. Karim entered the suite and did his customary morning greeting to any and everyone.

He walked into his office. Unlike most of the financial advisors, who preferred the large wooden desk, Karim went for a more streamlined look with a large glass desk and a chrome credenza. A black leather sofa sat on the far wall by the window overlooking downtown Atlanta's skyline. Pictures of Lisa and Dominic were scattered here and there. His degree and a few awards and certifications hung on the wall over the credenza in chrome frames.

Karim plopped himself down into his chair and lifted the phone to check his messages.

"Karim, this is Camille Harris and I wanted to talk to you about the acquisition. We need to get this thing while it's hot. Please call me at . . ."

"Yeah, yeah, yeah," he said, jotting down the number of a woman who was rich as a Rockefeller and trying to buy a majority stake in an arena football league.

Beep.

"Karim, this is Leo, the got-damn Lion. I was calling to check up on ya' drunk ass. Give me a call back. Maybe we can go check out those sorry Hawks tonight. Holla at your boy."

Beep.

"Karim, this your big bro'. I'm calling you from a cell phone but don't call it back. I missed you on Saturday. I hope to see you this weekend."

A frown found Karim's face. Something in his brother's voice didn't seem right. Something outside of the typical disappointment from his missing a visit. Now he really felt bad about not forcing himself to take the two-hour drive up to the Georgia State Prison, where his brother would be for the rest of his life.

Karim looked around his office until his eyes found the sheepskin hanging on his wall.

KARIM SPENCER
MASTER'S OF FINANCE

A hell of a sacrifice for you, he thought.

He flipped through a pile of mail that had been placed on his desk. Mostly junk. Then he found the one piece he was looking for.

"Jackson and Wiley, Attorneys at Law" was stamped in the upper left-hand corner.

"Sorry-ass lawyers," he thought, anticipating the worst.

Mr. Spencer,

We regret to inform you that the request for early release for Omar Spencer has been denied. If you would like for our firm to continue the appeals process, please notify us in writing within thirty days of this letter.

Randy Jackson, Esq.

"You bastards couldn't defend an innocent man if he was accused of a crime in Iraq," he said, balling up the paper.

The telephone rang and Karim snatched it up.

"Mr. Spencer, you have a Leo Harris on line one," Heather, his perky little secretary, said.

"Send him through."

The line beeped.

"Black man," Leo said. "You still wanna fight?"

"Sorry about that, bro'," Karim said, a little embarrassed about his drunken behavior the other night. He hated it when he allowed his demons to get the better of him.

"It's all good," Leo said. "Do you need to talk about something?"

"Nah, just had a few too many, that's all."

"Okay. You know I'm here for you, man," Leo said. "Guess what?"

"What?"

"I think I got a sex problem. I couldn't get nobody on the phone last night and damn near lost my mind. I had to jack off."

"I'm not hearing this on *my office phone,*" Karim said, throwing hints that he knew Leo wouldn't catch.

"What's wrong with your phone? You want me to call you on your cell?"

"You know, you can be an ignorant ass sometimes."

"Who you talking to, boy?" Leo snapped.

"You, ya fat bastard," Karim snapped back.

"I got your fat bastard right here in my pants."

"That's gay, and you're now an official suspect of the down low."

"That shit ain't funny, man. Don't be playing like that," Leo said.

"Who said I was playing?"

"Anyway, I'm headed off to Paris."

"What's going on in Paris?"

"Nothing. Vacation. I need to see if French pussy is any different than American pussy," Leo said.

"You a mess."

"I hope it comes with a lot less attitude."

"Let's meet over at Twist in Buckhead," Karim said.

"Why we can't go see the Hawks?" Leo asked.

" 'Cuz they suck."

"Man, you one of them fair-weather fans, man," Leo said.

"Whatever."

"How did everything go with your nephew? With his fine-ass momma. Karim, when you gonna hook a brother up?"

"I'mma hook yo' ass up with a black eye."

"Man, whatever. I hooked *you* up."

"That's because I'm a good guy. You're a hoe."

"Man is not meant to have one damn woman. That shit is unnatural."

"Is it?"

"Hell yeah. Biologically it doesn't make sense. A woman gets pregnant, her ass out of commission for damn near a year. What the hell am I supposed to do for a damn year?"

"I don't know, bro'," Karim said, going through some paperwork and only half listening.

"What's up with JaQuan?"

"He's out of jail. But something tells me it won't be his last time visiting the pokey. Nadiah wants him to come and live with me. *Not*."

"Why?"

"Man, that boy is off in thug-life fantasy world. I mean I might pick him up sometime this week and take him to the barbershop. Damn hair looks like he's homeless," Karim said.

"Him living with you might not be a bad idea for him. He could use that positive male influence."

"Why don't I send him to live with *you,* then?"

"Send him on. Him and his momma. We can be a family." Leo laughed.

"You'll send both of them back in less than a day."

"Man, I'll have JaQuan's li'l ass on the straight and narrow in no time. Lemme tell you how to handle a kid like him," Leo said. "Every time he says something halfway crazy, punch him in his got-damn mouth. Bam. I'm talking about knock the shit outta him. Harder than a muthafucka. See, you got to try and knock his wisdom tooth loose."

"Shut up, Leo."

"Twist?" Leo said. "Why you always wanna go to those bougie-ass places, Karim? Just 'cause you got one of them fancy suit-wearing jobs don't mean you gotta hang with the stuffy crowd."

"We can't go to Jazzy J's every night. We are too old to be ducking bullets, homey," Karim said.

"Shiiiiit, it's better than dealing with those little prissy girls you like. I had me one of those little things before. She couldn't fuck worth a damn because she was too busy worrying about how she looked. That's why I like me a ghetto slim, somebody who will threaten me with bodily harm if I don't put it down right. Those li'l chicks with college degrees be boring as hell. Aww, ohhhh, yes, yes. That feels very well," Leo said in a feminine high-pitched voice. "Give me some broken Ebonics. Ya know. Somebody who's happy with a number-six combo at Wendy's. I spend twenty dollars and I'm knocking the screws out her ass."

Karim sorted through more e-mails while Leo went on his tangent.

"Karim. Karim," Leo called. "Man, whatchu doing?"

"I'm at work, boy, what do you think I'm doing?"

"I'm sitting here trynna give you some life lessons and you working for the man. Damn sellout."

"It's official: you're retarded. I'll see you later," Karim said, hanging up the phone on one of the best dudes God ever created.

Leo Harris was a three-hundred-and-fifty-pound personal trainer and the brother of the woman he called his. How he got that job, big as he was, was a mystery to all below the clouds. And he had a huge client base. Crazy but true. Maybe it was his thousand-watt smile that won his clients over.

They'd met at a Victoria's Secret fashion show at the Fox Theater in downtown Atlanta ten years ago. It was the hottest ticket in town, and Karim had an extra ticket due to some girl canceling out on him at the last minute.

Karim figured he'd use the ticket to impress a new female, but then he saw Leo trying to sneak in. He almost died of laughter when he noticed Leo's extra-large frame trying to ease under the velvet rope while the security guard was distracted.

Karim walked over just as the security guard turned and caught him. He had Leo penned up against the wall.

"Whoa, whoa, he's with me," Karim said, handing Leo the ticket.

"Man, I thought you were inside," Leo said, trying to play it off as if he knew Karim.

"Nah," Karim said, playing right along with him.

"Thanks, bro'," Leo said once they were away from the guard.

"Not a problem. Enjoy yourself," Karim said after shaking the big man's hand.

Karim disappeared into the crowd and after a few minutes of mingling, he found himself standing by the bar talking to one of the many attractive women who were all over the place.

Leo walked in between Karim and his new lady friend.

"I owe you one, potna," Leo said in his down-home Georgia accent.

"Nah, we're good. Go on and have yourself a good time," Karim said, trying to get back to the company of this Naomi Campbell look-alike.

"No sir, I know a good favor when I get one. What you drinking?" Leo insisted.

Naomi huffed and gave Leo a nasty look.

"Damn dog," Karim said, rethinking his decision to give this man the ticket.

"Damn dog nothing. I owe you a drink and doggonit I pay my debts."

Naomi gave Leo one last evil eye and walked off.

"Now you owe me one for real," Karim said as he watched the long-legged stallion disappear through the crowd.

"Trust me. I did you a favor. That chick ain't nuttin but a

project gold-digger. You can do better. Now, what you drink-ing?" Leo said, getting the attention of the bartender.

"I don't drink," Karim said, pissed off.

"You see that chick you were talking to name is Tiara. And trust me when I tell you, she's about as shysty as they come. Up in here trynna play high post," Leo said, turning and leaning on the bar. "She cleans up good, though."

"What do you mean, shysty?"

"She was only trynna get in your pockets, potna," Leo said.

"Ain't nuttin' in my pockets but lint, dog," Karim said.

"Yeah, right. Tickets for this party cost a grip."

"Those tickets were free. I'm a student and broke as a joke."

"For real?" Leo said. "Well, youngster, you're gonna have to use your resources a little better. You could've sold those tickets for a few hundred a piece."

"For real?" Karim said with a frown. He was already kicking himself for that slip-up.

"Yeah, but I certainly appreciate the kindness. And that's on the real," Leo said, biting his lip as a gorgeous specimen walked by.

"Damn," Karim said.

"Damn is right. That bitch is fine as frog hair."

"I ain't talking about these women, I'm talking about that money I could've had."

"Don't sweat it. It's only money," Leo said. "You know, I haven't seen one ugly chick in this place."

"That's the truth," Karim agreed as he took in the roomful of beautiful half-naked women.

"Oh, and not only is Tiara a gold-digger," Leo said, turning around with a beer and a bottle of water. "She has that package, too."

"What package?" Karim asked, taking the bottle he was offered.

"That package that be putting dudes to sleep with a nasty cough. She's H to the izz I, V to the pizz I," Leo sang. "HIV-positive every day of the week. Worse than that, I heard she trynna give it to cats."

"She needs to be locked up then," Karim said, watching the woman he'd planned to bed as her long legs strutted across the floor and up to the next man. "I guess we're even."

"I got somebody you can meet. It's my sister Lisa. She's a sweetie, so don't get fucked up."

They shook hands, and that seemed to seal their bond.

———

Karim signed a few papers and returned a few phone calls. He was uneasy and felt like he needed to get out of the office.

He looked up at the clock on his wall. It was only ten o'clock. He picked up the phone and dialed Lisa's number at work.

"Hey baby," she answered.

"What are you doing?"

"Headed off to a meeting," she said.

"Okay, I won't hold you. I just wanted to tell you that I was gonna run by the center and pick up Dominic. We're gonna ride out to see Omar."

"Will you make it back before dinner?"

"I think so, but if we're gonna be late, I'll call you."

"Okay," Lisa said. "Tell Omar I said hello and ask him if he received the card and pictures we sent."

"Okay. Love ya," Karim said, hanging up the phone.

Karim walked over to his assistant and told her he was going to be out for the rest of the day.

He took the elevator down to the lobby and bumped into Mariah.

"We have to stop meeting like this," she said.

"True."

"Are you leaving early to make up for coming in late?"

"Nah, gotta go and take care of some business."

"Okay, take care," she said as she strutted away.

Karim stopped and watched her as her long legs strutted over the marble floors.

Damn, that's just not fair, he thought. *One woman should not be that fine.*

Karim shook off his lust and headed to his truck. Then he called Leo.

"What's up, black man?" Leo said.

"Guess who's trynna holla at your boy?"

"Who?"

"You know that long, tall drink of water you met last week?"

"Mariah?"

"Oh, you remembered her name?"

"Hell yeah. How could I forget? I fuck her all the time."

"What?"

"Damn right. Masturbate to her every night."

"Too much information. Anyway, she gave me that look."

"What look?"

"You know that look."

"Oh *that* look," Leo said. "Well, she's your type."

"So is Lisa."

"Are you smoking? Lisa ain't going nowhere, fool. That's my sister and I love her to death, but damn that. You better hit that."

"You crazy. How you gonna encourage me to cheat on your sister?"

"Y'all ain't married. But even if y'all were, fuck it. Like I said, it's unnatural for a man to be with one woman."

"You need to move to Africa. I'm good."

"Oh see, now I know you got some real deep-rooted problems going on in your dumb-ass head. Lisa is the bomb girl and all, but you can't pass up no ass like that, fool. That's top-of-the-line coochie. Even I can admit to that one. Bougie, fine and rich. You better try to break her damn back."

"It's something about her that makes me a little weak. I gotta admit that."

"Yeah, fool. It's called new pussy. Listen. If you hit it, you don't have a problem. Lisa will never find out. I know I ain't telling her. Well, unless you don't hook me up with Nadiah— then I'm telling every damn thing."

"Let it go."

"Damn, you selfish. But listen, if you don't hit it, then that's a problem, because fine women don't go for that turn-down shit. She'll be on your case every day. She becomes the predator and you become the prey, and you know our asses ain't cut out to be chased by no fine woman. We'll fall down and get caught on purpose."

"Man, 'bye. I gotta go get my son. We're headed out to the prison."

"A'ight. Tell your brother I said what's up. But listen to me before you go. My advice, find you a nice little quiet spot in that building and try your best to knock a screw out of her back. Don't take her to no nice hotel. She used to that. You gotta get ghetto with her. Slap her on her ass and call her some fucked-up names. Bougie chicks like to be treated like that sometimes."

"Advice noted, Dr. Leo."

"You're welcome."

Karim smiled and hung up the phone. That boy was a special case. He drove toward his house with his mind on Mariah's long legs.

Just as he turned into his subdivision, he had to swerve to miss something lying in the middle of the street. Karim pulled over and put his truck in park. He slowly walked up to . . . Senior.

"Senior," he called slowly as he approached.

"What up, Dad," Senior said, popping up but still seated on the ground. "I'm trynna get a tan, yo."

"A tan? You already black enough. You're gonna get run over."

"For real, Dad?"

Karim looked at the man and all he could do was feel sorry for him. Senior had on a pair of boxer shorts, hiking boots, and a sweat band. His other clothes were folded up under his arm.

"The sun shines real good right here, yo," Senior said standing up. "Let me hold a few dollars, Dad."

Karim reached in his pocket, pulled out a few singles; he handed them over to Senior.

"Thanks, Dad."

"Senior," Karim called. "Don't lay in the street anymore, man. Go lay on my deck if you want a tan. The sun shines real good back there too."

"Okay," Senior said before walking down the street in his Timberland knockoffs and too-large boxer drawers.

Karim got back into his vehicle and drove through the subdivision toward the day care to pick up his son.

7

Nadiah heard the sounds of children's laughter. She popped her head up from her laptop and saw two little girls walking with their backpacks bulging from beneath their winter coats.

"Good morning, Miss Nadiah," one of the little girls said.

"Good morning, Sierra," Nadiah said back. "How you doing in school?"

"Good. I got all A's on my progress report."

"That's good. And how are you this morning, Miss Kimberly?"

"I'm fine. I got all A's, too."

"Well, that's good. Y'all bring them report cards over and let Momma Mae see 'em and she'll give you something good."

Nadiah missed her school days. She'd always loved school and done well. Once upon a time she had big dreams, but then she had JaQuan and those dreams were permanently deferred.

"Good morning, Nadiah," Romeo, a friend of JaQuan, said. "How you doing?"

Romeo was everything she wanted her son to be. He was smart, respectful, and a star athlete headed off to the University of South Carolina on a football scholarship.

"I'm good. How are you doing in school?"

"I'm straight. You coming to my game on Friday?"

"I might. Who do y'all play?"

"St. Pius."

"Okay, I might check you guys out," Nadiah said.

"JaQuan doing okay?"

Nadiah frowned.

Romeo smiled knowingly. "Tell him I said what's up. Coach is always talking about him and how fast he is. He should've never quit the team."

"I know," Nadiah said.

"Well tell him I said what's up. You take care," Romeo said as he ran off to catch the bus.

Nadiah stood on the porch and stared at Romeo. He was the son of a drug-addict mother and a no-show father, yet he'd overcome all of that and was headed off to play college football at a very good school free of charge. She watched until all of the school kids were on the bus, then she walked into the house and headed for JaQuan's room.

Nadiah stood over her son while he slept. Standing there looking down at him, she couldn't help but feel ashamed. As much as she hated to admit it, her son was one sorry little boy, which meant if something didn't change, he would be one very sorry man one day.

The power of deoxyribonucleic acid was incredible. JaQuan had never met his father, yet he acted and looked just like the man. His dark chocolate complexion, large nose, and almond-shaped eyes were the spitting image of his father. She could understand the physical resemblance, but how he could inherit being shiftless was beyond her.

Nadiah hated to admit to herself that she was allowing her son to be just like his sperm donor, a hustler who never met a shortcut he didn't like. Standing there looking down at her son, she couldn't help but hate the feeling she had growing inside for him. Normal kids were off to school, yet hers lay on the bed sleeping his life away. Something had to change.

"Get up," Nadiah said.

JaQuan stirred.

"Get up!" Nadiah yelled.

"Hunh," JaQuan said, stirring a little more.

"Get up."

"Why?" JaQuan said, rolling over on his back.

"Because I said so," she snapped.

JaQuan slowly rose on one elbow and stared at his mother.

"Don't you lay your lazy behind up there staring at me. Get up."

"Man," JaQuan said with a frown before lying back down and pulling the covers over his head.

Nadiah snatched the covers off him. He snatched them back. She went into the kitchen and returned with a glass of cold water. She pulled off the covers again and poured the water on him.

"Get your ass up," Nadiah growled.

JaQuan jumped up from his bed as if he'd been bitten by a snake. He looked at his shirt, which was now drenched, and glared at his mother.

"You better get your ass . . ."

"Man, you keep on trying me and you gonna get dealt with," he said in a menacing tone.

"Dealt with?" Nadiah said, easing over to her son, who towered over her.

"You heard me," JaQuan said, still fuming.

She reached up and slapped him. When she reached back again, he grabbed her hand. She tried to pull away, but her son was way too strong.

"If you don't let my arm go . . . ," Nadiah started.

"What?" JaQuan said, roughly shoving his mother away.

Nadiah stumbled back into the dresser before falling to the floor.

She was shocked.

Hurt.

Dismayed.

This couldn't be happening. Something had to have come and possessed this boy in the middle of the night.

Nadiah pulled herself up and ran back at her son, arms whaling. She hit him with every ounce of her being. In his face, arms, back. She punched, kicked, and clawed at the eyes of her own flesh and blood.

JaQuan covered up and tried to push his mother away, but this time he was no match.

"Hey!" Momma Mae shouted from the doorway. "What the hell is going on in here?"

Nadiah wouldn't be denied her due. She kept on punching and kicking, all the while screaming words that would make a sailor blush.

Momma Mae walked over and shouted again. "Nadiah," she said, holding her heart.

Nadiah backed away, her chest heaving as she tried to catch her breath.

JaQuan was no longer her son. He was a stranger for whom she just happened to be responsible.

"If you think for one second that I'm going to let you put your hands on me, you got another thing coming," Nadiah screamed.

"Wait a minute," Momma Mae said. "What's going on in here?"

"She came in here and jumped on me while I was asleep," JaQuan said, holding his face and head. "I was just sleeping and she came in here throwing water on me."

Momma Mae looked at Nadiah with a quizzical look.

Nadiah ignored her grandmother and glared at her son. Blood was running down his face. She wasn't sure where it came from, and at this point she couldn't care less.

"Get dressed," she barked at JaQuan. "Now you can either go to school or take your disrespectful little ass back to jail. And if you *ever* raise your hand to hit me again, I will kill your black ass," she said as she stormed out of the room.

Nadiah walked into her room and slammed the door. She sat on the side of the bed and placed her head in her palms. She wanted to cry, but she couldn't find the tears for a son who had crossed a sacred line.

When she lifted her head, Momma Mae was standing over her.

"Nadiah," Momma Mae said.

"Not now. I can't hear you right now," Nadiah said.

"No, chile. I ain't here for that. I want you to know that you're a better woman than you let on to be sometime," Momma Mae said, sitting down beside her granddaughter. "If any of mines ever raised a hand to me, it would've been their last. When I walked in that room you was on the floor. Now either you're clumsy or that boy has lost his mind. You did the right thing. Only thing is, you should've done it a long time ago."

Nadiah dropped her head.

"It's tough for a woman to raise a boy to be a man. We can do it, but that still don't make it easy. I did it and women been doing it for ages, but it's a different day now. Too many bad elements in the world today. Something has to be done with him. And jail is not the answer," Momma Mae said.

She stood and placed a rare but comforting hand on Nadiah's shoulder and gave her a slight squeeze.

"Momma, I . . . I . . . I . . ." Nadia stopped, at a loss for words. "I asked Karim if he could take him and he said no."

"He's not Karim's chile. You can't keep pawning him off on people. That's why he feels the way he feels about you."

"I don't pawn him off on nobody," Nadiah said.

"Oh really? Well who kept him for two years while you moved to New York to try that acting thing? Who kept him for another two years while you joined the band and ran up and down the highways? Then when you made it back, you moved him into a house with some man you barely knew. When that one didn't work out, one month later, you moved in with another one. That didn't work out so you found another one. How do you think his momma running around jumping from man to man made that boy feel? You ever thought about how he must've felt with you giving all your attention to some man? He never felt first in your life. A child needs his momma to be there. Daddies can go, but momma should always be there. It's easy to beat him up but he's already hurting. He's hurting bad, too. That's why he's acting out," Momma Mae said before walking out of the room.

Nadiah looked at her grandmother as the truth hit home like never before.

8

Central State Prison wasn't very scary-looking. It was a far cry from the last place Omar Spencer was housed. It took some crafty legal maneuvering and lots of under-the-table money for Karim to get a convicted murderer placed in a low-level prison like Central.

There were no menacing guards standing in fifty-foot towers with fingers on triggers. No barbed or razor wire keeping the inmates from an easy escape.

Karim drove down the long, winding road toward the prison and stopped at a little white shed with a guard inside.

"Good afternoon," a guard at the entrance said.

"Got yourself a little co-pilot today."

"Yeah, decided to let him beat up on his uncle for a few," Karim said as a second guard walked around the car with a mirror attached to a long stick. The guard walked around the perimeter of the vehicle with the mirror, looking at the under-carriage of his truck.

The gate opened, and Karim was waved through.

"Enjoy your visit," the guard said.

"Thanks."

The next checkpoint was at least a hundred feet away where he went through a similar search, only this time a dog was with the guard.

Karim walked around to the back of his truck and un-buckled his son's car seat.

"Daddy, where are we?"

"A bad place," Karim said.

"Bad people in there?" Dominic asked with wide eyes.

"Most of 'em are, but there are a few good ones in there by mistake."

"Is Uncle Omar bad?"

"Nah," Karim said, lifting his son into his arms. "He's one of the good ones."

They walked into a lobby and through a metal detector. Karim nodded at a friendly guard as they were led into a room where lawyers spoke with their clients.

A few minutes later, Omar walked in.

Omar was about five feet ten inches tall, and his hair came all the way down to the middle of his back. He wore a white shirt and white pants with a blue stripe down the arm and leg. His prison number was stenciled across his chest pocket.

Karim stared at his older brother and didn't know what to think.

"Heyyyyy," Omar said, hurrying over to pick up Dominic. "Look at you. You're growing like a weed, boy."

"Hey, Uncle Omar," Dominic said.

"How are ya, big bro'?" Karim said, shaking his brother's hand and pulling him in for a hug.

"I'm okay," Omar said, still holding Dominic. "This little fella here is something else. He looks so good. Lord have mercy. I'd give anything just to take him to the zoo."

Karim dropped his head.

"You gonna take me to the zoo?" Dominic asked.

"One day," Omar said, taking a seat.

"So how are you holding up?" Karim asked as he took his own seat across from his brother.

Omar hunched his shoulders. "Ten down, a life to go."

"I'm working on that," Karim said.

"I know you are," Omar said with a smile and a pat on the knee. "You been drinking your water?"

"Yeah, man."

"You a lie."

Karim smiled. Omar was always good at detecting his untruths.

"You better drink water, boy. Water cures all kinds of woes and illnesses. Cleanses the body like nothing else."

"I'm gonna do better."

"Does your daddy make you drink water, Dominic?"

"No. His breath was stinky in the morning time," Dominic said.

Omar laughed. "Well then, your daddy needs to drink water and Listerine."

"Both of y'all shut up," Karim said.

Omar couldn't stop laughing.

Karim watched him. He knew beneath the smile there was a man fighting for his sanity. It pained him that he couldn't do more to help his brother, but the court system was slow as molasses and worked slower than a snail crawling through molasses when it came to appeals.

"Don't you stress yourself out behind me," Omar said, still trying to take care of his little brother. "I'll be okay."

"How's Manuel?" Karim asked.

Omar jerked his head back and sucked his teeth.

"What?" Karim asked.

"Can I say A-hole?" he whispered. "Getting on my nerves to the tenth degree."

"Man, if you gonna go through all that drama you might as well get a woman," Karim said.

"Daddy, can I color Uncle Omar a picture?" Dominic asked, climbing down from his uncle's lap and onto an empty chair.

"Ohhhh, I would love that," Omar said.

"Sure, man," Karim said, opening up his briefcase and pulling out the book and crayons he'd packed just for this occasion.

"I don't know if you noticed it or not, Karim, but this is a males-only prison. So getting a woman in here might be kind of hard. Besides, I don't judge who you sleep with, so stop judging me."

"Fair enough," Karim said, throwing up his hands.

"So how's everything at home? Oh, tell Momma Mae I

said thanks for the food. Everybody in here wanted a piece of that sweet-potato pie."

"I'll tell her. Lisa wanted to know if you received whatever it was she sent you."

"Tell her I said thank you. She's a sweet girl. When you gonna make an honest woman out of her?"

"I don't know."

"How's the baby girl?"

"Crazy. She moved back home," Karim said, shaking his head.

Omar smiled. "One day that girl is gonna be rich. She certainly does her own thing. How's JaQuan?"

"Trying his best to get up in here."

"What?" Omar said.

"He got locked up last week. I had to take Nadiah over there to get him out. And you should've seen him. Acting all thugged out. I wanted to kick him in his head."

"Tell me you're kidding! Please tell me this is some kind of joke you're telling me! For what?"

"He wants to be a pimp."

"A pimp?"

"Yep."

"You tell that little buster that pimps in here get pimped. Tell him I said find something constructive to do and sit his little butt down somewhere. Ohhhh, I can't believe that," Omar said.

"Believe it. Now Nadiah has found the nerve to ask if he could come and live with us. Yeah, right."

"And what's wrong with that?"

"Man, I don't have the patience for JaQuan. He's trying his best to be the black KKK. You know, one of those little dumb bastards running around terrorizing good black folks. Half of these little fools don't care about getting locked up because they worship some ignorant rapper who romanticizes the life. They think it's cool because Fifty Cent made a video in a jail cell," Karim spat, shaking his head.

Omar leaned back in his chair and folded his arms. "Why can't he come and live with you?"

"That boy is off the chain. I mean, when you look up the word 'nigga' in the dictionary, you'll see his picture. Nappy hair, shiftless, lazy, pants hanging off his butt. He's been kicked out of every school he's been enrolled in because he refuses to act right. I mean he literally personifies the word 'nigga' to a tee."

"Well, unniggerize him then," Omar barked.

"If I had a magic potion, I would."

Karim watched as his brother's face transformed into a demonic frown.

"Karim," Omar said. "I made a helluva sacrifice so that you could do good things. And I expect you to do just that. Not just when it's convenient, but all the time. And especially with your own blood."

"But . . ."

Omar held up a silencing finger that cut Karim off. "It's your duty to keep that boy from ever stepping foot in a place like this. Because if he does, then you will answer to me and trust me, this ain't what you want."

Karim sighed.

"The next time I see you, I want to hear good reports about JaQuan. He needs to be back in school even if you have to take your butt up there and sit down with him. You will not give up on that baby. And you will bring your little tail down off of your high horse and stop judging people. Who do you think you are? People do what they feel they need to do to get by, and just because you wouldn't do like that doesn't mean a damn thing."

"Man, what about Dominic? I can't have JaQuan over there influencing my son with his foolishness."

"I'm going to pretend I never heard that," Omar said. "Because a real man does the influencing. A real man can handle a little boy, not the other way around."

Karim lowered his voice. "When I look at him, I see them. I can see their faces just as clear as day. It's as if they are him."

"You know what? I see their faces every day too, but I deal with it. Do I wish I could turn back the hands of time and do things a little differently? Absolutely. But I can't. What's done is done. So you need to figure out a way to get over that," Omar said. He rose to his feet.

"Sit down, man," Karim said, trying to calm his brother. "We just got here."

Omar reached over and looked at the picture Dominic was coloring. "That's nice. Can I take it with me and finish it in my room? That way it'll be like we worked on it together."

"Okay," Dominic said, handing the half-done picture to his uncle.

"Family should always work together," he said, rubbing

Dominic's head and shooting Karim a disdainful glare before
he walked out of the room.

———

Karim sat there staring at the door after Omar had left. He
felt like crap. He looked around at the plain white walls and
realized that it should have been him going back to his cell.

———

Karim was only seventeen years old and a senior in high
school when his girlfriend, LaDonna, became pregnant. Even
though neither of them had any real means of supporting
their child, Karim was ecstatic. The baby came, and they
named the boy Ziar.

Two years later Karim was a sophomore at Clark Atlanta
University, and any and every chance he got he made his way
over to Bowen Homes Projects, where LaDonna lived with
Ziar.

Then, one Saturday, everything changed. Karim was sitting in the living room watching college football as LaDonna
played outside with two-year-old Ziar.

The screams were deafening. Karim jumped to his feet
and ran out of the apartment just in time to see a black
Mercedes-Benz screeching away. He caught a quick side view
of the passenger's face as they made their getaway. A police car
with sirens screaming was hot on their trail.

Karim arrived by his girlfriend's side to find her on her
knees clutching a now lifeless Ziar, who had been hit by the
driver of the Mercedes.

Karim's body shook when he looked down at the body of his son. He closed his eyes and asked God to save his child, but he already knew that God had taken him home. He knelt down beside his girlfriend, who was now soaked in the blood of their child, and screamed a heart-wrenching howl.

A police car pulled up and stopped. Two officers got out, and both of them rushed over to where Karim and LaDonna were kneeling with their son.

An ambulance showed up sometime later.

The police asked around but true to the code of the streets, no one was talking to them. "Stop Snitching" T-shirts were everywhere, and for some strange reason people were willing to let a child's murder go unsolved before they would talk to the police.

Karim couldn't sleep, study, or eat. He was thoroughly disgusted with his so-called people for their lack of cooperation with the police about the murder of his son. Karim called Omar, and they took to the streets themselves.

———

Karim forced the thoughts of yesteryear from his head and looked at his son.

"Daddy loves you, man," he said, pulling his little one into a tight embrace.

"I love you too, Daddy," Dominic said.

Karim thought about his high school sweetheart LaDonna and what the death of their child did to her. Standing witness to the horrible crime proved to be too much.

She was okay until the funeral. Seeing her child lying in a

tiny casket drove her over the edge. She screamed for the last time right before Ziar was lowered into the earth. A day later, she was committed to Georgia Regional Mental Facility.

Karim thought about what Omar had said. He had to help his sister with JaQuan. The thugs who killed his son were long gone; now he had to figure out a way to bury their ghost. Nadiah needed his help, and he couldn't believe he'd turned her down.

"Come on, little buddy," he said to Dominic as he packed up his briefcase.

"Daddy, is Uncle Omar coming home today?"

"Not today, but soon."

"He looks like a girl," Dominic said as he followed his father out of the room.

"Yeah, I know. But he's all man," Karim said as he motioned for the guard to let him out.

9

Nadiah waited on the front porch for her cab. Today was going to be the first day of the rest of her new life. She had tried many times before to get her life in order, but some man always found his way into the picture and she found herself latching onto him, hoping he was going to solve all of her problems. She knew better now.

"JaQuan," she called. "Come on."

JaQuan trudged his way outside.

"Where we going?"

"It's up to you," Nadiah said. "We can go to school or we can go to jail, but you're not gonna lie around here and do nothing."

"Whatchu care?"

"What?"

"You ain't been caring. Why you care now?" JaQuan said with nothing but contempt oozing from his every word.

"Boy, I don't have to explain nothing to you. You're a child," Nadiah said. "And you don't pay no damn bills."

"That's all it takes for you, Momma? Somebody to pay your bills? That's all you worth?"

Nadiah felt like slapping him again, but she restrained herself.

The cab blew its horn.

"Come on," she said, walking down the steps.

JaQuan looked at his mother but didn't move.

"JaQuan," Nadiah said, stopping at the foot of the steps. "If you don't bring your little . . . If you don't come on, I swear to God I'm calling the police."

"Call 'em. I don't care. I'd rather be locked up than to stay with you any day," JaQuan said as he walked down the steps.

Nadiah reached out to grab him, but he jerked away and took off running down the street.

"JaQuan," she called. "JaQuannnnnn!"

JaQuan never looked back.

"You keep on running with your dumb ass," she yelled, "and don't you bother coming back."

Nadiah wanted to scream all of her frustrations away, but instead she took a seat on the bottom of the stairs. She closed her eyes and ran her fingers through her short Afro to try and relieve some of the stress that was threatening to blow a blood vessel in her head.

This teenage crap is for the birds, she thought.

Momma Mae stood in the doorway behind a screen and watched her granddaughter.

"You know all that name-calling ain't necessary," Momma Mae said before turning around and walking back into the house.

The cab driver blew his horn.

Nadiah didn't look up.

The driver blew again.

"Ma'am," he yelled out of the window. "Did you call a cab?"

Nadiah couldn't speak. She shook her head and he pulled off.

A familiar black pickup truck pulled up and stopped.

It was Nick.

"Can I speak with you for a minute?" he said, standing outside the driver's side door and talking over the roof of his truck.

Nadiah stood and walked over to him.

"When you coming home?" he asked, ignoring her tears.

Selfish as ever, she thought.

"I *am* home," she said.

"Come on, baby. I promise you if you give me one chance to prove myself, we'll be happy. Just got beside myself and that will never happen again."

Nadiah stood there looking at him. He was black as the night was long, tall and strong. He was so beautiful, and right now she could really use his strong hands to hold her up.

"You put your hands on me," Nadiah said.

"I didn't mean that," Nick said, shaking his head.

"What *did* you mean?"

"I was frustrated about being laid off, but they called me back to work so everything is good."

Nadiah's eyes narrowed to little slits.

"Come on, baby. We gonna be a family," Nick said, putting a little jewelry box on the hood of his truck. He opened it up and a sparkling ring sat inside. "I wanna make you an honest woman."

Nadiah's heart raced.

She had never been proposed to before. She had to force herself from reaching out and grabbing the ring.

"Yeah, baby. I spent a nice little chunk of change on that rock right there. But nothing but the best for my baby."

Nadiah stood there staring. The ring was one of the most beautiful things she had ever seen.

"Come on, baby, get it together," Nick said, smiling from ear to ear. "I know that thing blinging but it got you tongue-tied."

Nadiah took her eyes off the sparkle and stared at Nick.

"I think I'm going to have to pass."

"Pass?" Nick asked, surprised.

"What's gonna happen the next time you get laid off?"

"Baby, all I can say is that what happened the last time won't happen again. Come on home. Let me show you," Nick pleaded.

Nadiah looked away. She sighed and turned back in the direction in which JaQuan had run off.

"I'm thirty years old. My spanking days are long gone. You take care of yourself, Nick," she said as she turned on her heels and walked back up the driveway.

"Okay," Nick said, flipping from sweet to sour in an instant. "You gonna regret this. I mean, what do you bring to the table anyway other than a piece of pussy? I can always get that. Ghetto bitches like you come a dime a dozen," he yelled. "A dime a got-damn dozen."

Nadiah smiled. "Well, go get you one. I hope she likes your little dick."

"Yeah, whatever," Nick said. "Your sorry ass couldn't get enough of it. You ain't nuttin' but a hoe. A stripping-ass hoe."

Not too long ago, his harsh words would have cut her to the core. Maybe it was because deep down inside she felt she was those things.

But not now.

It felt so liberating to be able to ignore him.

Nadiah was so lost in the moment that she didn't see Nick racing up behind her. She turned around just in time to see his large hand coming toward her throat. He wrapped both of his hands around her neck and threw her to the ground like a rag doll.

"Oh, you don't know who you dealing with," Nick said, standing over her.

Nadiah tried to get up, but he grabbed her by the back of her shirt and threw her down again.

A gunshot exploded.

"The next one won't be in the air," Momma Mae said, holding that long gun that was almost bigger than her. "It'll be in your ass."

Nick jumped back, holding up his hands.

In an instant, the bully became the victim.

"I . . . I . . . I . . . ," he stuttered.

"I . . . I . . . I . . . Hell. You better leave from 'round here, boy, while you still can," Momma Mae said, walking down the steps.

Nick backed away with his hands still up until he reached his truck. He jumped in and sped off.

Nadiah was on the ground, still catching her breath.

Momma Mae turned and walked over to her granddaughter.

"Come on, chile," she said. "Get up. I swear you stay in some mess."

A fusillade of emotions overtook Nadiah's mind. She was hurt, embarrassed, and thoroughly disgusted with herself for once again choosing the wrong kind of man, but when she stood up there was a weird smile on her face.

"You been watching too many Tyler Perry movies," she said.

Momma Mae looked at her granddaughter strangely. "Girl, you been smoking that stuff again? Man out here going upside your head and you smiling?"

"No," Nadiah said, shaking her head. "I ain't smoking. Just feels so good to know I'll never see him again."

"Did he have a little dick for real?"

Nadiah put her index finger and her thumb about an inch apart and they shared a laugh.

10

JaQuan sat in the basement of his friend Marcus's house. The walls were covered with magazine pictures of hip-hop artists. The floors were covered with dirty rugs, and the place reeked of animal urine from Marcus's pit bull terrier.

On the floor was a pee-stained mattress and for some reason, being there reminded him of his short stint in jail.

Marcus passed JaQuan a forty-ounce bottle of Olde English beer and started rapping into a makeshift microphone:

> *I be a trap star in the making,*
> *Bonafide hustler, 'cuz niggaz be faking*
> *Hit the block hard to get that dough*
> *I really want a Caddy with the butterfly doors*
> *Pockets stay swole, Yeah I'm on my grind*

24/7 pimping nuttin' but dimes
Killing comes easy 'cuz I don't care.
Penitentiary bound. I'm America's nightmare.

"Man," JaQuan said, nodding his head. "You need to put that on a CD and sell it, shawty. That was fire."

"That's what I'mma do. Soon as I get this money right. See, I got a plan, shawty. I ain't out here buying no damn clothes for these hoes. I'm saving my dough for these flows. Ya heard? Oh, that shit rhymed—I need to write that down," Marcus said, running to get a pencil.

"Boy, you a fool," JaQuan said, laughing at his homey.

"You know when I blow up, I'mma put you on right," Marcus said.

"I can't rap. What I'mma do?"

"You can help me fuck my hoes. You'll get paid just for that. Certified hoe tester. I'm telling you, shawty, this thing gonna happen. It got to," Marcus said, shaking his head. "It got to. I gotta get rich, shawty."

"Why you need to be rich?"

"Man, that's a dumb-ass question. So I can shine nigga and never hafta ask another nigga for nuttin'."

"True," JaQuan said, thinking about how he could throw all of his cash in his mother's face. She didn't think he was going to amount to anything, but he knew better.

"That's what I'm talking about," Marcus said. "Man, the first check I get I'm going to the dealer. Fat-ass ride with some twenty-eights on that bitch."

Marcus was only a year older than JaQuan but he was already a hardened criminal. Six of his sixteen years on this earth were spent behind Georgia prison bars.

"Speaking of hoes," Marcus said, taking the forty from JaQuan. He took another big gulp and half the bottle was gone. Then he handed it to JaQuan. "This hoe I met was 'posed to be bringing another freak over here."

"Man, I ain't got time for no hoes," JaQuan said.

"What else you got to do?"

"I gotta find me a place to stay."

"You must be scared of pussy," Marcus said.

"Whatever. I don't see how I'mma be scared of something I'm in all the time," JaQuan said, taking a drink.

"You a fool with yours," Marcus said, slapping JaQuan's outstretched hand. "You got some money?"

"Nope. Where I'mma get some money from?"

"I thought your fine-ass momma might've gave you a few dollars."

JaQuan didn't like hearing that, but he didn't say anything.

"You wanna make some quick money?" Marcus asked.

"I'm down," JaQuan said, eager to put himself in a position where he didn't have to depend on his mother.

"Check this out," Marcus said, producing a ziplock bag filled with a hard whitish-yellowish-looking substance.

JaQuan looked up at Marcus. Marcus was a true hustler and the girls were crazy about him. He was one of the best rappers in the neighborhood, and once his demo tape got in the right hands he was gonna be doing it big. JaQuan could feel it. Something told him to stick close to his friend.

"What's that? Crack?" JaQuan said, trying to act as if this wasn't his first time seeing the drug.

"Nah, crystal meth," Marcus said with a sly smile. "White folks' drug of choice. I got put onto this in the pen. I'm telling you, this shit sells itself. All you gotta do is take it to the geekers. White folks spend money, shawty. Please believe it."

JaQuan stared at the little bag.

Marcus was watching him.

JaQuan looked up and caught Marcus's stare. He didn't like what he saw. He couldn't put a finger on it, but something told him if he accepted his friend's offer, he could never turn back.

"Yo, man, you think your mom will let me camp out here tonight? My mom's tripping 'bout that school shit," JaQuan said, changing the subject.

"Man, fuck school. All them years of listening to all that nonsense just to get a job. Nah, 'cuz I'll take my chances in the streets. Yeah, you can stay. I don't give a shit. See, I got it good. My mom don't even care if I go to school. She know the deal. Long as I bring that money home she's good."

JaQuan nodded his head, but he couldn't have disagreed more.

"So whatchu gonna do, homey? Barbecue or mildew?" Marcus said, nodding at the little bag.

JaQuan took a deep breath and handed the bag back to Marcus.

"You scared?" Marcus said with a smirk and a sly smile.

"Nah," JaQuan replied. "Just ain't ready to go there."

"Well, shawty, you gonna have to do something to get your paper."

JaQuan nodded. All of a sudden reality hit him. He was in new territory now. He couldn't stand his mother, yet he didn't want to do what it took to stay away from her.

"I'm out," JaQuan said, popping up. "I'll holla at you a little later, man."

"Where you going?" Marcus asked. "I told you I got them hoes coming over here."

"Man, if it's the same ones from the other night then, I'll pass. I can't believe I got locked up behind those ugly-ass chicken heads."

"Shawty, you gotta learn the game if you gonna play it. I swear you hustling backwards," Marcus said, laughing. "You got to be the only pimp who gets locked up before his hoes."

"Who said I was a pimp?" JaQuan said. "And I ain't got no hoes."

"That's for sho'. A real pimp would've told those undercovers where they could kiss. You gonna point out the hoes," Marcus said, laughing hysterically before mocking JaQuan. " 'Oh sure, Mr. Undercover Policeman. If you give me twenty dollars, I'll lead you right to the hoes.' You gotta be kidding me. That was dumb as hell."

JaQuan heard some talking coming down the stairs. Two girls walked down into the basement. He looked at Marcus and smiled.

"Yeah," Marcus said as if he had something to do with their bloodline. "Talk that ugly-girl smack now?"

"You straight," JaQuan said, eyeing the short one with the micro-braids. The taller one wasn't bad either, but she had a gold tooth and that wasn't cute.

"This my man JaQuan," Marcus said, introducing him. "This LaQuela and Nicole."

"Nicole," JaQuan said, looking at the short girl.

"Oh, she the only one you see?" LaQuela said, nodding her head with a smile.

"Nah, what's up witcha?" JaQuan said, reaching out to shake their hands.

Marcus lit up a blunt and passed it around. Everyone took a puff except Nicole.

"Got a little something to help get this party started," Marcus said as he reached in his pocket and handed out small pills. "It's that X, baby."

"Ouuuu wee," LaQuela said. "You know these things makes me horny."

"And talkative," Marcus said, handing one to Nicole.

She looked at him like he was crazy.

Marcus glared at her. "Oh, you one of them stuck-up broads," he said as he removed his clothes, then plopped down on the pee-stained mattress, naked as the day he was born.

LaQuela got undressed and lay beside him.

JaQuan wasn't going to be outdone. He stripped out of his shirt but stopped when he looked at Nicole, who was only standing there watching.

"Man, y'all hurry up. What y'all trynna do, make love under the moonlight and shit?" Marcus said.

"I'm out of here," Nicole said, gathering her things.

"Well, get the hell out then," Marcus said.

"Don't worry," Nicole said, walking up the steps.

"You leaving, Nicky?" LaQuela asked as she rolled over on top of Marcus.

"Yeah, and you need to come with me," Nicole said as she hurried up the steps and out of the house.

LaQuela looked after her friend, already feeling the effects of the ecstasy pill.

JaQuan pulled his shirt back over his head and followed Nicole.

Once they were outside, JaQuan saw her running across the street. He gave chase and caught up with her.

"You okay?" he asked as they stopped on the corner.

"I'm good," she said. She kept walking.

"Can I talk to you for a second?"

"I'm not interested in talking to dudes on drugs."

"I'm not on drugs. It's not like that."

"Did anyone ever tell you that weed is a drug? Besides, I could've sworn I saw you pop a pill."

JaQuan smiled and opened his hand. He had faked taking the pill.

"Okay," Nicole said, unimpressed. "That only means you're not man enough to tell your friend that you don't want his drugs."

"Nah," JaQuan said. "It's not like that."

Nicole stopped walking and looked at JaQuan. Her eyes met his.

"JaQuan," she said. "Our worlds are too far apart."

"Why you say that?"

"Look at you," she said. "You hanging out with a drug dealer and too scared to tell him you don't want to take his pills. What grade are you in?"

"Ninth," JaQuan said. Normally he would lie and tell girls he was in the tenth, which was where he was supposed to be.

"And you are how old?"

"Don't worry about it," JaQuan said, walking back to the house.

"JaQuan," Nicole called.

JaQuan picked up a light jog but stopped dead in his tracks when he saw four police cars pulled up in front Marcus's house. Officers jumped out and ran up on the porch and around to back of the house.

Nicole's eyes popped open. "I gotta go get my cousin," she said, running off toward the house.

JaQuan grabbed her.

"No," he said. "What you think those cops gonna do if you run up in there? They gonna lock you up too."

They eased across the street, a little farther away from the house. A few minutes later, they watched as Marcus and LaQuela were led out in handcuffs.

"I hope she learns her lesson. Always running around behind some wanna-be thug," Nicole said.

"I'm glad I wasn't in there. I just got out of jail."

Nicole looked at him with a frown. "For what?"

"Hanging out with that fool," he said, watching his friend standing in the cold wearing only a pair of boxer shorts and handcuffs.

"You need new friends," Nicole said.

"You might be right."

"If hanging out with your man got you locked up, then I know I'm right."

"It was a mistake," JaQuan said.

Nicole turned to him. "So now you're making excuses.

You seem like a cool guy, JaQuan, but . . . never mind. You take care," she said, walking away.

"Hey," JaQuan said, running after her. "Wait up. But what?"

Nicole kept walking. She gave him a look that said "Do you really need to ask?"

"I'm just saying, that's my man, but I don't hang with him like that."

"What school do you go to?" she asked.

"I go to Columbia," he lied. "What about you?"

"Redan."

"Okay. So you gonna give me your number?"

"Give me yours and I'll call you."

JaQuan gave Nicole his number at Momma Mae's house and reached out to give her a good-bye hug. She stopped him and reached out her hand instead.

He watched her until she disappeared around the corner. Just like that, he was sprung.

11

Karim sat in his truck in the garage nursing a big white bottle of Grey Goose vodka. Every time he came back from seeing Omar he felt worse than he had before he arrived. Lately things were getting even worse. He just couldn't shake it off; his past stayed with him, haunted him. Now he was seeking a reprieve in a bottle.

His cell phone rang and he looked at the caller ID. It was from his job. He let it go to voice mail. Once he heard the beep, he called his service and played the message back.

"Karim, this is Jack Brown," Karim's boss said. *"I need an update on the Camille Harris purchase. What's going on? I need an update as soon as possible."*

Karim grimaced at the thought of missing another hearing on the case. "Shit," he said, slamming his hand on the steering wheel. "Pull it together, Karim."

He flipped open his phone and called his boss back.

"Jack. Karim Spencer. How are you?" Karim said, trying to mask his drunkenness. "I'm on the case. Waiting to hear back from this auditor out in Texas. Seems like it's a go from the numbers I pulled. I'm in a meeting right now with my kid's teacher, but I should hear something in the morning and I'll keep you posted."

"Thanks. Her people are saying we're dropping the ball. You're very good at what you do, Karim, and I don't need to tell you what this could do for your career. I personally picked you for this, so I hope you don't let me down."

"Absolutely not. I'm on it."

"Good. Give your daughter my best," Jack said, hanging up before Karim could respond.

Karim flipped the phone closed.

"It's *son*. I have a son, you fat bastard. I have pictures of him all over my got-damn office. If you got off of your fat ass sometime and got to know who the fuck works for you instead of cashing in on hours you don't have anything to do with, you'd know that. I have a son. Two of 'em," he yelled at the phone loud enough for his boss to hear him fifty miles away.

Lisa walked outside and around to the driver's side just as Karim was taking another swig. She pulled open the door.

"Karim," Lisa said. "Why are you out here screaming?"

"Leave me alone," Karim snapped, trying to pull back the door.

"No," Lisa said, snapping right back. "What is going on with you?"

"Nothing." He was pulling the door, but Lisa stood in front of it. "Lisa, move out of my way."

"You're drunk. It's six o'clock in the evening and you're drunk."

Karim reached up and hit the garage door opener. As the door rose, he turned on the ignition.

"You better move," he said.

"I'm not moving anywhere," Lisa said, reaching across him to turn off the ignition. She tried to remove the keys but Karim grabbed them. He turned the truck back on and put it in reverse.

What neither of them knew was that Dominic had followed his mother outside and was hiding behind the truck.

Mother's intuition kicked in and at the last second, Lisa looked back to see her son's hands go up to grab the truck's bumper.

"*Stopppppppp!*" she screamed, causing Karim to slam on the brakes.

His world stood still.

He heard LaDonna's scream mixed with Lisa's.

Lisa ran behind the truck and picked up Dominic, who was on his bottom, crying. She held him close as tears made their way down her cheeks.

Karim jumped from the truck and ran to the back. He ran his hands all over his son, trying to make sure he was okay. He tried to pull him away from his mother, but Lisa wasn't having it.

"What is wrong with you? You could've killed him," she said, her voice cracking.

Karim stood and stared down at the woman and child. He backed away. He grabbed his head with both hands and moaned in agony as his demons of a dead son, an unjustly incarcerated brother, and a schizophrenic first love took their toll on him.

Karim stood there and watched as Lisa stood up and carried Dominic back into their house.

He jumped into the truck and slowly backed out of the driveway.

12

It was three o'clock in the morning and Nadiah was on the porch again. The weed smoke was blowing in the cool November night and she was feeling real mellow. Somehow she had managed to push most of life's stressors out of her head for a few hours in order to focus on her book.

JaQuan was still in there, though. Every two or three minutes she would think about him and his whereabouts. How was he doing? What was he doing? Was he even alive? That was the one question that caused her the most pause. The streets were tough, and she knew in her heart that he was a house boy acting out his rap video fantasies. He was far from prepared to deal with the element of society who made the streets their playground. They could see him coming from a mile away.

Nadiah tossed the thoughts away and started typing again. She reread the last line a few more times before rewriting it. *There.*

A smile creased her face.

Then her nerves kicked in.

She couldn't believe it. She had just typed the last period of her novel.

Momma's a Virgin was done.

Nadiah leaned back in her chair and stared at the laptop's computer screen. She scrolled down, two hundred and eighty-eight pages.

A rush came over her like never before and she couldn't remember ever feeling this good.

She'd needed this.

Three years of hard work had finally paid off.

Nadiah put the blunt to her mouth but stopped before it touched her lips. She looked at the smoking cigar paper and put it out. There was no way she was going to ruin this real high with a manufactured one. She was no longer a nobody; she was an author.

She ran one last spell check and accepted or denied the changes. She couldn't believe it. This was major. People would read her work. Wait! What if they didn't like it? New nerves kicked in. *Oh my God, please let them like it,* she thought. Never mind that; she was feeling too good to let her negative thoughts interfere.

Nadiah closed the laptop and thought about another good feeling. Earlier today she'd caught a cab to Crane Academy for Girls in the ritzy section of Dunwoody, where her daughter Nakaria was a first grader. She stood outside the fence and watched as the beautiful little girl ran around on the playground with her friends.

Nadiah stood there watching her child until the bell rang to call the girls back inside. Nakaria lined up with her friends; then, right before she walked inside the building, she turned toward Nadiah and waved.

That one little wave opened up the floodgates. That one wave instilled in her a determination she'd never known existed to get her child back. Oh, how she missed her little girl! Yet as much as she hated to admit it, Raymond, her daughter's father, was the best thing for her at the time. But now things needed to change.

Nakaria was only six years old; therefore Nadiah still had time to become a good mother. And no one was going to stop her from doing that. The first thing she had to do was find a different job. The second thing was to get that damn supervised visitation order removed.

Nadiah looked at the cordless phone resting on the porch's rail. Something had to be done to change things, and the legal system wasn't on her side. She grabbed the phone and dialed Raymond's number. He was married, but his precious little wife would have to understand that this was important and if she didn't, to hell with her.

Raymond picked up on the first ring.

"I'm sorry to call your house at this hour, but we need to talk," Nadiah said.

"I'm up. As a matter of fact I was expecting your call. Thought it might be at a decent hour, but you never did things the way normal people did them."

"Why were you expecting me to call?"

"Kari told me she saw you at her school today. You know that is a direct violation of the court order, don't you?"

"Come on, Raymond, give me a break."

Nadiah could see Raymond now, sitting his pompous butt behind some big, fancy desk in his study, sucking on some pompous pipe, wearing some pompous smoker's jacket.

She could never figure out how the two of them had found joy in each other's company. They were polar opposites.

———

Even how they met was right out of *Men Are from Mars, Women Are from Venus*.

She was standing at the MARTA stop waiting on the 54 bus when a big white Maybach drove through a puddle, splashing muddy water all over her. She cursed the driver out. Then she saw the brake lights illuminate. The driver made a U-turn and then another. He stopped in front of her.

"Ma'am, did I just splash you?"

"You sure as hell did. Now my coat is ruined."

"Please," he said, reaching for his wallet. "Allow me to pay for the damage."

"Allow you? I got your license plate number memorized. I was planning on tracking you down."

The man smiled and handed her four hundred dollars and a business card. "Will that cover it?"

Nadiah looked at the money and calculated how much the coat had cost her. "Yeah, this will more than do it," she said, handing him two hundred dollars back.

"Keep it and give me a call so we can formulate a plan to

get you off this bus. You are far too pretty to be out here in this weather," the man said.

The bus pulled up.

"There's your bus. Would you like a ride?"

"Yeah, but I don't know you. Thanks for the money."

"No problem," the man said, spinning off.

Two days later Nadiah called him, and they became Friday date buddies even though she thought he was the world's whitest black man. For his part, he thought she was the worst black women had to offer. Loud, obnoxious, and expecting the world to give her something just because she was cute.

They changed each other. She learned that there was a different segment of black people who weren't sellouts just because they wanted a better life for themselves, and he learned to stop being so quick to judge and to pull his drawers out of his ass. And then came the sex, followed by Nakaria.

———

"I know what the order says, but I want to see her," Nadiah said.

"You do see her," Raymond said.

"Once a month in a public place is not good enough. I want to see her alone. Without you lurking around in the background like I'm on some kind of visit in a prison."

"Is that how it is in prison?" Raymond stabbed.

"I wouldn't know," Nadiah retorted. "She's my daughter, and I would never hurt her."

"Okay," he said. "You hurting her was never the problem.

You making sure she doesn't hurt herself, well, that's another story. You surrounding yourself with people who won't hurt her is certainly a concern."

"Oh, come on, Raymond, you know that was an accident. I didn't know that man was doing drugs. How many times do I have to tell you that?"

"I've heard it far too many times. I'm not concerned about him. He can overdose on the crap for all I care. It's you that I have the problem with. *Parenthood 101*. It's a great book; you should buy it. The first principle is, be mindful of the company you keep. Your mistake could've cost Kari her life. And I will not take that chance again."

Nadiah thought back to that day four years ago. She was dating a hustler named Kenny. Kenny got drunk one night and carelessly dropped a small package of cocaine on the floor. Nakaria found the drugs and chewed up the package. Nadiah found her daughter crying hysterically and throwing up on the living-room floor.

An ambulance was called and the police soon followed. Nadiah and Kenny were both arrested on child cruelty charges.

After two days in jail, Nakaria's father paid a lawyer to free Nadiah with an understanding that she would sign over full custody of their daughter to him.

"You have no idea how much I regret that day, but I can't make it go away. If I could, I would. Please, Raymond, let me see my baby. Let me get to know her."

There was a long pause on the other end of the phone.

"I'd like nothing more. She needs to know her natural mother."

Nadiah's heart raced. Was he saying what she thought he was?

"But! What's changed? How is your son? Is he doing well in school?" Raymond asked.

Just like that, Nadiah's heart sank back down into the pit of her stomach.

She knew Raymond. The minute they got off the phone he would set the wheels in motion to find out JaQuan's status in life. The results wouldn't come back positive.

"He's a teenager. Going through it," Nadiah said.

"Do you have your own place?"

"I'm back home."

"So you are telling me you want me to subject my child to a gun-toting grandmother who sells liquor out of a back room as a source of income?"

Nadiah could feel her daughter slipping farther and farther away from her.

"See, here's the deal," Raymond said. "I don't mind you seeing Kari. As a matter of fact, I wish you were the kind of mother who was able to provide a positive and nurturing influence in her life, but . . ."

"I can do that."

"I don't want to be the villain here, but you're still not ready to be in her life. Once you get your life in order, give me a call."

"Raymond," Nadiah said.

"Yes."

"I'm trying here. I really need to spend some time with her alone. Even if it's only for an hour."

"Are you still dancing?"

"Raymond, please."

"Answer the question."

"No."

"When did you stop?"

"Does it matter?"

"Yes. What do you do for a living?"

"I'm looking for a job right now."

"Well, when you find one, call me."

Nadiah heard the dial tone. She wiped away the tears and pushed the end button on the phone.

Then she sat back and cried for all that life was putting her through. In some strange way, she felt she deserved everything she was getting.

Nadiah heard something rustle in the distance and her heart skipped a beat. She looked across the street and saw what appeared to be a man hiding behind a bush.

Nick.

Damn it, she thought in a panic.

Nadiah quickly grabbed her computer and tried to rush into the house before he could do something to harm her.

"Ma," the voice said, stopping her in her tracks.

It was JaQuan.

"What are you doing out here this time of morning, boy?" she said, overjoyed that he was all right.

JaQuan didn't say a word. He just walked up the driveway and walked past her into the house.

"JaQuan," Nadiah called.

Once again, she was ignored, but that was okay.

For now.

13

Karim sat slumped over at a table in the back of Café 33 in Buckhead.

"He's back there." Moe Kelly, the owner, pointed toward the back of the bar. "I think he's had one too many to be driving."

"Looks like he had ten too many," Leo said, looking at Karim.

"He was talking crazy a little while ago. Something about how he's not a good guy. All kinds of crazy things. So I took his keys. Found your number in his cell phone. Sorry to bother you at this hour, but I figured you wouldn't want your boy out there like that."

"Nah, I'm glad you called."

"A'ight, well, I'm about to close up, so if you need some

help getting him to the car just holla," Moe said, nodding before he headed back behind the bar.

"Thanks, Moe," Leo said, walking back toward Karim.

Leo took a seat across the booth from Karim. He didn't say anything.

Karim looked up. "What?"

Leo still didn't say anything.

"What the hell are you looking at?"

"Karim," Leo said, running his fingers together. "What's going on? You don't even drink, yet all of a sudden you're getting plastered. Now, I may not be the brightest bulb in the chandelier, but even I can see that something's not right. You're acting like the end of the world is coming."

"It is. At least the end of my world."

"Don't talk like that. Anything can be worked out. Anything," Leo said. "What's going on?"

Karim sighed and shook his head. "You want a drink? I'm buying."

"The place is closed, man. I came to take you home."

"What time is it?"

"Four in the morning, man."

"Is it?" Karim said, peering at his watch. "Damn. I know Lisa is worried sick."

"She is," Leo said, nodding his head.

"Well, she might as well get use to me not being around."

Karim thought about his last episode with Lisa. The thought of running his son over made him want to commit suicide. He really didn't feel like he was fit to live.

"Oh man," he said, close to tears.

"Karim," Leo said. "I'm your friend to the end, man. Just tell me how I can help you."

Karim stared blankly over Leo's head.

"I don't know."

"If you don't want to tell me, then go and talk to somebody. There is nothing wrong with that, ya know. Black people get on my damn nerves scared to talk to a therapist."

"I don't need to talk to nobody, man," Karim said, standing up on wobbly legs. "I know what I need to do."

"Moe," Leo called out.

"Yeah," Moe said from behind the bar.

"Let me get them keys?"

Moe tossed the keys to him and looked on with a caring eye. "You fellas okay?"

"Yeah. I appreciate you, bro'. We'll get out of your hair now."

"What hair?" Moe smiled. "Karim, you take care of yourself, buddy. Life kicks us all in the ass at one time or another. Real men kick back."

Leo helped Karim out to his truck. He placed him in the passenger seat and buckled him in before walking around to the driver's side.

"Where's your car?" Karim asked.

"At your house. Lisa dropped me off here."

Karim dropped his head.

"Now one of two things is gonna happen. You'll either get some help or I'mma whip your ass. I'm getting sick of this shit. Why you gotta get that damn drunk?"

"Kiss my ass, you overweight mutha . . . ," Karim slurred.

"You can go to hell. I don't need you. I don't need anybody except my sons. Everybody else can go to hell."

"Sons," Leo said. "How many kids do you have, Karim?"

Karim fanned him off and pushed the lever to lay the seat back.

14

Nadiah stood in line at Kinko's with her 2GB flash drive. She couldn't believe how good she felt. Even with all the drama with her son and not being able to see her daughter, she felt good.

Momma's a Virgin was done.

It was more than just a book. It symbolized a new direction in her life. It gave her a sense of purpose. It motivated her. She pulled out her cell phone and called Lisa.

"Lisa. This is Nadiah. Do you remember I asked you a while back if you would edit my book?"

"Yes," Lisa said as if she wasn't interested in talking.

"Well, I finished the book," Nadiah said with a huge smile on her face.

"That's great, Nadiah."

"Okay," Nadiah said, already tired of the dead voice on the other end. "Now I didn't expect you to be as excited as me, but damn. Who stole your tampons?"

"I'm sorry, Nadiah. I have a lot on my mind right now."

"Is everything okay?"

"No. What's going on with your brother?"

"What do you mean?"

"All of a sudden he's been drinking a lot and acting weird."

"Since when did Karim start drinking?"

"That's just it. He doesn't drink. That's how I know something is going on. He almost ran Dominic over yesterday because he was too drunk to see what he was doing."

"What?" Nadiah asked, her voice rising.

"Yeah. Do you know anything? Have you talked to him? Did he share anything with you?"

"No," Nadiah lied. She had a real good idea what was bothering her brother.

"Okay," Lisa said. "Send me the book in an e-mail. I'll get on it right away. I need something to take my mind away from the drama around here."

"Okay," Nadiah said, as she added her big brother to the list of stresses in her life. "I'll send it tonight when I get home."

"Okay."

"Is Karim there now?"

"No. You think he's cheating on me?"

"What?" Nadiah said. "Please. Be real. First of all, I don't think he has it in him, second of all—"

"Oh, you wouldn't tell me anyway. You're his sister, and blood is thicker than water. He's normally home by now."

"Stop worrying before you give yourself an ulcer. Karim will be okay," Nadiah said, just as she caught the eye of a tall, sexy man in a suit.

"Thanks, Nadiah."

"Kiss my nephew for me."

"Okay."

Nadiah hung up the phone and tried to act as if she didn't see her weakness standing only ten feet away. Tall, dark, and handsome was not a good combination for her. At least not at this stage in her life. But damn, this man looked like he'd just stepped out of the screen of a Beyoncé video.

He's coming over here, she thought.

"Excuse me," Pretty Boy said. "I know you from somewhere. I know that sounds like a line, but it's not."

Nadiah gave him a courteous smile but didn't say a word. Most Atlanta men knew her from Magic City's Gentleman's Club, though she never gave them the time of day.

The man placed a finger to his forehead and rubbed his temple. "Man, I wish I could think right now. I swear I know you, and when I say it you'll be like, 'Oh yeah.' "

"I don't know," Nadiah said, stepping up in line.

"Do you read poetry at the The Grand on Old National on Thursday nights?"

"Sorry, wrong chick," Nadiah said.

"I'm Victor," he said, extending his hand.

No, not again, she thought.

"I'm Nadiah," she said, taking his hand without a smile.

"Let me give you a card. You really should think about modeling."

Oh, he's a corny ass. "You think so."

"Absolutely. You have very strong yet soft features," Victor said, handing her the card.

"Thanks."

She looked at the card. *Victor Hanson, photographer.*

"So maybe we can talk over a photo shoot sometime," Victor said, licking his lips LL style.

Corny but smooth. "I don't know. I'm pretty busy and I'm not vain enough to be a model," Nadiah said.

"What do you do?"

Nosey li'l something, ain't he? "I'm an artist. I just finished my first book. I'm here to get it bound."

"You wrote a book?" Victor asked, excited.

"Yeah." Nadiah couldn't help but smile.

"What's the title?"

"Momma's a Virgin."

"Momma's a Virgin? That's an interesting title. What's it about?"

"Long story," Nadiah said.

"My sister's best friend works for Random House in New York. I'm not sure what she does, but she works there."

Random House? This man's gonna mess around and make me fuck him, Nadiah thought, then quickly tossed the idea.

"Is that right?"

"Yeah. I'll tell you what. You agree to do a photo shoot with me and I'll use my contact to get your book in the door."

"Listen," Nadiah said, looking at the card. "Victor. I'm in a bad place in my life right now. So excuse my French, but men are full of shit. Let's be real. Why would you help me?

You don't even know me. You wanna have sex with me. Since you've been standing here you've done nothing but molest me with your eyes. You can't keep your eyes off of my breasts."

Victor seemed stunned.

"Nadiah, you're wrong. No doubt, you are a beautiful woman but I'm as straight as six o'clock. I would be lying if I told you I wasn't attracted to you, but that's neither here nor there. In my line of work, a pretty woman is easy to find. In all honesty, I was only trying to help a sister get to where she needs to be. That's all. Nice meeting you," he said. "I'm sorry you took offense."

"No need to apologize."

"Take care, and good luck with your book."

"Thanks," Nadiah said.

Victor reached out his hand. Nadiah shook it and he was gone.

Nadiah walked up and handed the guy behind the counter her flash drive.

"That's my pride and joy, so take care of it," she said.

"Cool," the young guy said.

"Also, do you have a job application?"

"Sure," the guy said, reaching under the counter and handing one to her.

While Nadiah waited for her book to be bound, she took a seat in the corner and filled out the application. She hadn't filled out one of these things in years. But she had to get Nakaria back. Once she was done, she walked it back to the counter and turned it in.

"Here ya go."

"That was quick," the guy said, scanning the sheet. "When are you available for an interview?"

"Anytime."

"Okay, I'll be in touch."

"Thanks," Nadiah said, with a strange feeling that he wouldn't.

She went back to the corner. She pulled out her cell phone and called the house.

"Hello," Momma Mae answered.

"Hey Momma. What is JaQuan doing?"

" 'Round there watching TV."

Nadiah breathed a sigh of relief. The last conversation with Raymond had given her even more incentive to be a better mom.

"Can you tell him to pick up the phone?"

"Hold on."

"Hello," JaQuan said.

"Hey. You okay?"

"Yep," JaQuan said with as much dryness as an old peanut-butter sandwich.

"I think we need to talk. I'm not going to curse and scream and I don't want you to get defensive. You're a smart boy, JaQuan, but you have to learn the world doesn't dance to your beat."

"It don't dance to yours either."

Nadiah took a deep breath. God knows she wanted to cuss this boy out.

"I know, but I'm grown, so I don't have as much to lose as you. Now we have to get you back in school."

"I gotta go," JaQuan said, hanging up the phone without waiting for a response.

Nadiah held the phone in her hand and wondered what she could possibly have done that would make her son hate her so much.

15

Karim woke up to his woman standing over him. His son wasn't around, and he jumped up reaching for him.

"Where's Dominic?" he asked, looking around wild-eyed.

"In his room. He's taking his nap."

"What time is it?" Karim asked, pulling himself up.

"Karim, you are going to talk to me and you are going to talk to me right now. I've tried to let you have your space, but now it's starting to affect this family."

Karim sighed. He looked at the woman who allowed him to breathe again.

"I got a lot on my mind, Lisa."

"Not going to do it. You're not blowing me off anymore. You don't even drink, then all of a sudden for the last couple of weeks you come home inebriated out of your mind. So much so that my brother has to bring you home. That is crazy."

"I know, but it's not gonna happen again."

"Your job called, and whoever it was didn't sound too happy."

Karim cursed as he thought about missing another meeting on his latest multimillion-dollar acquisition.

"Karim, I don't like being in the dark. Now, I can be as supportive as I need to be, but this is not working. You cannot keep trying to drink away whatever is bothering you."

Karim nodded. He stood and walked over to the dresser and pulled out a letter. He handed it to Lisa and sat back down on the side of the bed.

Lisa opened the envelope and read the contents.

She lifted her head and stared at her man. She walked over and sat down beside him.

"So this is what's been eating you?"

"Yeah," Karim said.

Lisa put her arm around him and kissed his cheek. "I know how much you love your brother. I'm sorry to hear that he lost his final appeal."

Karim started to open up, but he couldn't.

"I'm sorry about the way I've been acting, but Omar . . ."

"I understand," Lisa said. "But please don't drink anymore. My father is an alcoholic, and when you drink it scares me."

Karim nodded his head. His love for Lisa was second only to that of his son.

"I have to go to the mall. You wanna go?"

Karim looked at her and twisted his lips.

Lisa smiled. "I'm taking Dominic. He needs new shoes."

Karim nodded. "That boy's feet are growing like weeds."

"He's gonna be a big boy like his daddy," Lisa said, kissing Karim's lips before disappearing into the bathroom.

Karim walked down to the kitchen and got a drink of orange juice. His mouth felt like someone had stuffed it with a thousand cotton balls. He thought about his last conversation with Omar and picked up the phone to dial Nadiah.

"Hello," she said.

"What's up?"

"Nothing."

"How's JaQuan?"

"Why?"

"Because he's my nephew and I wanna check up on him. Is that a crime?"

"Nope. Just not you."

"You still want him to come and stay with me?"

Nadiah went silent.

"Hello," Karim called.

"I do, but I'm not trying to pawn him off anymore. Maybe that's the problem. We never really had any time to bond."

"Well, maybe y'all can get to that later. He needs a little firmness right now."

"So why you doing this now, Karim?"

"Just had to put things in perspective, that's all. He's just as much my responsibility as he is yours. So if it's cool, I'mma go scoop him up."

"Okay," Nadiah said. "When?"

"In a few hours."

"Okay."

Karim could tell she was struggling with the situation. She'd asked for it, but now that she was faced with it, she wasn't so sure. He ignored his feelings.

"See ya in a bit."

16

"Go pack," Karim said to JaQuan the minute he walked into Momma Mae's house.

"Pack?"

"Did I stutter?"

"Pack for what?" JaQuan said, still seated in front of the television with his feet propped up.

"You're going with me. Now get up and get your clothes ready."

"Man, I ain't going out to no Stone Mountain. I got beef out there."

"Okay, let's get this thing started off on the right foot. I call the shots. I give the orders and you follow them. It's a dictatorship for now. And my way is the law. Ya feel me?"

"No," JaQuan said, still seated.

"JaQuan, you're gonna lose. Now I'm not going to ask you again to get your little butt up and gather your things."

Momma Mae and Nadiah stood in the doorway watching.

"Man, y'all trippin' hard," JaQuan said, getting to his feet and walking back to his room.

Karim turned to Nadiah. "Now listen. If I'm going to do this, I don't wanna hear a peep from you. That may sound harsh, but I don't give a damn. That boy is spoiled rotten and between you and Momma Mae, he'll never get better."

Nadiah sighed and looked down. "Can I at least come and see him?"

"What are you talking about? He's not in jail. All I'm saying is if I make a decision, then it's final. Your way wasn't working, so let's try mine."

Nadiah nodded. "I don't want to see my son locked up ever again, Karim. That did something to me to see him like that."

"It should've," Karim said, reaching over and rubbing his sister's shoulder. "It did something to me too."

"I don't think it did anything to *him*. He didn't seem bothered at all."

"Did she tell you JaQuan hit her?" Momma Mae said.

"He did *what*?" Karim's eyes bulged.

"Knocked her right on her ass."

"He didn't hit me. He pushed me, and I took care of that," Nadiah said.

"Okay. I got something for Mr. JaQuan," Karim said.

"I owe you for this one, big bro'. Big time," Nadiah said with a smile.

"You don't owe me a thing, little girl," Karim said, looking at his watch.

"Stop calling me a little girl."

"Stop acting like one then."

"There you go."

"Man, where is this boy?" Karim said. "JaQuan," he called. "Hurry up."

Karim shot a glance over to the fireplace and noticed the picture was gone. He wasn't sure how he felt.

"I'll be outside."

Karim's cell phone rang the minute he stepped back into his truck.

"Hey, baby."

"Hey," Lisa said. "Where are you?"

Karim was silent.

"Hello?"

"I'm here."

"Is everything okay?"

"Nah, not really. Baby, we're going to have a houseguest."

It was Lisa's turn to become silent.

"JaQuan's been acting out and he needs a little intervention."

"And what do you think you're going to do?" Lisa asked.

"I don't know, but I told Nadiah that I would take him and try to help him," Karim said.

"I mean, I'm all for helping people, but Karim, you can't go making decisions like that without at least speaking with me first."

"I know and you're right, but . . ."

"But he's still coming?" Lisa said.

Karim exhaled. "I can't just leave him over here with Nadiah."

"That's Nadiah's kid. You may think you can save the world, Karim, but you can't."

"And I'm not trying to. Just JaQuan. If I don't do this, he's gonna die or end up in jail. I don't want that," Karim said.

Lisa went silent.

"Okay, Karim," she finally said. It was clear that she wasn't happy, but she was always supportive of her man. "I was calling to tell you I was gonna order some wings. I don't feel like cooking. I guess I'll order a few more."

"Thanks, Lisa. And tell Dominic I'm on my way."

"All right," she said. "I'll see you guys in a few."

Karim hit the end button on his phone and thought about the task he had just agreed to tackle.

He looked up and saw his nephew coming toward him with a large black garbage bag filled with what he assumed were clothes.

Karim got out of the truck and walked around to open the trunk. JaQuan tossed the clothes in the back of the cargo area without a word and walked back into the house. A few seconds later he returned with another big black garbage bag.

That's some damn luggage, Karim thought.

"You ready?" Karim asked.

No answer as JaQuan got in the truck.

"Put your seat belt on. And you need to know one thing, JaQuan. I'm not crazy. I don't talk to myself, so if I ask you a question, I expect an answer."

"I'm ready, man," JaQuan said with wrinkled brows.

"Kill the mean mug, nephew. I'm not your enemy," Karim said, putting the truck in reverse. He looked up and saw Nadiah and Momma Mae standing in the doorway, looking as if their baby were being sold off into slavery.

Both of them were waving. He tapped the horn twice and headed home.

About half an hour later, Karim pulled into his driveway and pushed the button that raised the garage door. He slid his truck in right beside Lisa's BMW convertible.

"Welcome home," Karim said.

"How long I gotta stay here?" JaQuan whined.

"I don't know, JaQuan."

"I'm saying. Why'd I have to bring all my clothes?"

"Because you need a change of environment."

"Man, y'all blowing this thing way outta proportion. It was a misunderstanding, I'm telling you."

"What kind of grades are you getting?"

"I ain't in school right now," JaQuan said.

"Why?"

" 'Cuz them teachers be tripping, man. Talking 'bout I had some weed in the bathroom. They smelled weed and I was coming out of it, but I didn't have it."

Karim shook his head.

"JaQuan, the world isn't against you, man. But if you're out here wilding out, it'll seem that way. Now if you want a lifetime of jail cells and booty bandits, then I can't help you. But if you wanna make something out of yourself and live the right way, then you're going to have to trust me. I'm not a tyrant and neither is Lisa, but we have rules over here and I expect you to follow 'em."

JaQuan looked out of the window. The look on his face said that he would rather be in jail.

"Let's go," Karim said, getting out of the truck and walking to the back to retrieve the bags.

They walked into the house and Dominic ran to his father as if he hadn't seen him in weeks.

"*Daddddddyyy,*" he screamed, but he stopped in his tracks when he saw his cousin. "*JaQuannnnn.*" Dominic slid as he changed direction.

"What's up, li'l buddy?" JaQuan said, reaching down and picking up his cousin.

"You gonna go with me and my daddy to get some ice cream?"

"You want me to?"

"Yeah," Dominic said, excitement oozing from his little voice.

"Well I guess I'm going," JaQuan said, putting Dominic down.

"How you doing, JaQuan?" Lisa said, smiling as she walked over and gave him a big hug.

"I'm good," JaQuan said, dropping his head sheepishly.

"Are you hungry?"

"Starving."

"Well, put your clothes in the guest room and get washed up," Lisa said in her normal bubbly tone.

"Where's the guest room?"

Karim frowned. It was at that moment that he realized

how far he had removed himself from his family. Here he was living right across town and his own nephew had never visited his home.

"Upstairs to the left. Last room on the left," Lisa said.

Karim looked at Lisa, trying to read her. She busied herself in the kitchen as if nothing was out of the ordinary.

"Are you gonna be okay with this?" he asked.

"Don't have much of a choice, do I?"

"There *is* a choice. If you want me to, I'll take him back right now."

"And make me out to be the bad one? I don't think so. I'll be okay."

"No you're not."

"Yes I am."

"No you're not."

"Yes I am."

"If you're okay, then how come I didn't get a kiss?"

Lisa walked over and stood in front of him. She puckered her lips and stood on her tippy-toes.

Karim smiled and leaned down until their lips touched.

"I think what you're doing is a wonderful and selfless act. I just wish you would've spoken with me first. I mean, when my sister needed a place to stay I came to you. And you said no."

"You know that's not the same thing. Your sister is thirty-six years old with sixty kids."

"So," Lisa said smartly. "What are you trynna say?"

"That she needs to invest in some condoms. I would've been spending crazy money on hotels just to get some sleep."

"Whatever," Lisa said, setting the table for four. "JaQuan," she called out. "It doesn't take that long to wash your hands, boy. Come and eat."

JaQuan came down the stairs and scooped up Dominic in one fell swoop.

"What you doing, dude?" he asked the little guy.

"Playing with my car," Dominic said, showing the toy red Mercedes-Benz that he couldn't live without.

"You got some good taste, shawty."

"You talk funny," Dominic said.

"And you talk like a white boy."

JaQuan sat Dominic in a chair and took one beside him. Karim led the blessing and they dug in.

"Y'all always sit at the table for dinner?" JaQuan asked.

"Most of the time," Lisa said.

"So it's like Thanksgiving over here every day, hunh?"

"JaQuan, what do you want to be when you grow up?" Lisa asked.

"Play for the Falcons, but that don't seem like it's gonna happen," JaQuan said, grabbing a handful of chicken wings.

"Why?" Karim asked.

" 'Cuz."

" 'Cuz what?"

"I'm just saying."

"Saying what? First of all, you're going to have to learn how to complete a thought. Take your time and tell me what you want to do in life."

JaQuan looked uncomfortable. He looked down at his food and frowned.

"I mean, I don't know."

"And that's okay. You're only fifteen. But it's time you start putting yourself in a position to make something out of your life. Being a nigga is not gonna cut it."

"I am what I am," JaQuan said.

"So you think you're a nigga?"

"Yeah."

Lisa kicked Karim's foot to get his attention. Once he looked up at her, she shook her head for him to stop.

He got the message and left his nephew alone. He had plenty of time to get rid of that mentality. At least he hoped so.

17

Nadiah was no longer Nadiah. After sprinkling body glitter all over, applying eyeliner and lipstick, slipping into a skimpy thong bathing suit, six-inch stilettos, and a garter on her right thigh, she had miraculously turned herself into the stunning and tantalizing specimen the fans called Destiny. This was her last hurrah at this club. She didn't have any other prospects for a job, but she knew this wasn't it.

She stood on the stage overlooking the sea of black faces. She had the entire crowd in the palm of her hand. She was in control. This was the one place where she called the shots. Grown men stood with tongues hanging from their mouths as they mentally masturbated. The crowd was about sixty percent men, forty percent women. Atlanta was weird like that, and all the weirdos found their way into Magic City at one time or another.

Over the years, Destiny had danced for just as many women as she had men. She wasn't gay, but their money was green, so she took it.

The up-tempo song she'd requested came on. She wiped the pole down and started leaning with it. The crowd went crazy. Guys and girls rushed the stage throwing dollar bills at her as she did the moves to the latest crazy with a frown on her face.

Off came the top, and more dollars hit the stage. She walked from end to end as men and women tossed their hard-earned money at her like it grew on trees.

The song ended and a smooth ballad from Neo came on about some man being sick of love songs. Destiny was hands-down the finest dancer in the club and that was saying a lot, because Magic City had the best Atlanta had to offer.

She grabbed the pole and pulled herself all the way up to the ceiling and slowly slid down.

More dollars hit the stage.

Off came the bottom. And she placed her ass on the pole and slid up and down in a seductive manner.

I make it rain, I make it rain, I make it rain on them hoes, Li'l Wayne rapped.

Some dummy suffering from low self-esteem wearing a Tennessee Titans football cap and jersey came up to the stage and threw a wad of cash in the air. It had to be at least a thousand dollars in ones.

Destiny wasn't fazed. She didn't even crack a smile. Just kept doing her thing. Before long, she couldn't take a step without her stilettos landing on cash.

For her last song, which is what the people really wanted

to see, she called on an oldie but goodie, Prince's "International Lover."

Destiny made love to herself in such a manner that even the other dancers stopped to take notes. She rolled onto her back and arched it to the beat. Ran her hands slowly over her body, then rolled over on her stomach and pumped the stage's floor until the song ended.

Without reaching down on the floor for a single dollar, she stood and exited the stage to a standing ovation. Destiny was far too classy to be crawling around on all fours picking up money, so she paid a waitress friend of hers twenty dollars to do it for her.

As she made her way through the crowd toward the dressing room, everybody and their horny mother or father reached out to touch her. To congratulate her for making their night.

"Thank you, baby," she said over and over until she was out of their sight.

Two grocery-store-type trash bags filled with cash were brought to her.

"You always clean up," a waitress named Charrese said. "You should come in here more often."

"If I did that they wouldn't miss me," Destiny said as she slowly transformed back to Nadiah. "People always want what they can't have."

"You're my shero."

"Honey, you can find someone better than me to look up to," Nadiah said, handing the girl twenty dollars.

It was worth it to her to pay them to pick up her money. This club was full of fantasy, and she kept the illusion going that she was unobtainable. For the last two years, she hadn't done a table dance. Only the stage. After she got her earnings she was gone. Tonight it wasn't even eleven o'clock and she was headed home.

"I'm thinking about dancing. Seeing how quick you made all that money got me to thinking."

"Don't do it," Nadiah warned. "It's fast money, but you pay a heavy price for it. Trust me on that one. Go to school and get you a real job."

It took them a little under ten minutes to count all the ones. Some girls trusted the machine but not Nadiah. She only trusted the math she'd learned in school. Thanks to the fool in the Titans cap, she'd made out pretty good.

She walked the money into an office in the back, where the night manager was sitting behind a desk.

"Hey, Charlie. I need to change these ones," Nadiah said to the tall ex–NBA player.

Charlie grabbed a handful of the George Washingtons and placed them in a money machine. Once he was done, he gave Nadiah nineteen hundred-dollar bills.

"I might follow you out and rob you, girl," Charlie said.

"And get shot? It ain't worth it," Nadiah said with a smile. "Have a good night, Charlie."

"Hey, Destiny," Charlie called.

"Good night, Charlie," Nadiah said, already knowing where he was trying to go. He was about to offer her his salary for the next ten years in exchange for one night of her time.

She hated being at the club. She hated what she did for a living.

After she got dressed, she threw all of her things into her big Nike bag and headed back up the stairs. Most of the people didn't recognize her without all her Destiny gear, so she could slip out somewhat unmolested.

She stood in the lobby area of the club and called for a cab.

"I still wanna read your book," he said.

Nadiah's head jerked to the side. Not many people knew about her book. As a matter of fact, with the exception of Lisa, no one knew.

"Do you remember me?"

"Victor," she said. "It was only yesterday."

"True."

"So I guess seeing me here jars your memory."

"No. My daughter goes to school with your daughter. That's where I know you from."

Nadiah nodded her head.

"How's your little girl?" he asked.

"She's good. Thanks for asking. How's yours?"

"Good. We should get them together sometime. Maybe I can take some snaps of all of you guys."

"Persistent."

"I waited on your call. Do you still have my card?"

"I'm not sure," Nadiah said truthfully.

"Well, find it. I spoke with my sister even though you treated me like I did something to you. And she wants to read your work. She said her friend at Random House loved the title," Victor said.

"What's the title, Victor?" Nadiah asked with a skeptical look on her face.

"What is it with you?"

"I just think men are full of it and I don't like being played."

"*Momma's a Virgin.* I have no reason to lie to you," Victor said. "If you find the card, call me and I'll pass your book along. If not, good luck anyway."

Victor shook his head, paid his money, and walked into the club.

Nadiah walked outside and stepped into a cab. Something about Victor told her he was different. Or maybe he was just smoother than most of the guys she ran across.

Whatever.

She didn't have time for a man in her life right now. Even if lip-licking LL Cool J himself tried to holla.

Well, maybe she'd find time for LL.

18

"I like your nephew, yo," Senior said, standing in the twenty-five-degree cold wearing nothing but shorts and a bomber coat.

"You do," Karim said.

"Yeah, he cool people, Dad. He gave me a ride to the store last night. He cool, yo. Real cool."

"A ride?" Karim asked. "What was he driving?"

"Your wife's car, yo. That shit is fast, Dad. You spent some money on that one right there," Senior said.

Karim rubbed his temples. He did not just hear what he thought he heard.

"Are you sure it was my nephew, Senior?"

"Yeah, Dad. He was cussing you out for making him get a bald head. I told him it looked good."

"Thanks, Senior," Karim said.

Just when he thought his day couldn't get any worse, he hears this. It was bad enough that he'd just got fired. He had indeed dropped the ball on the Harris acquisition and damn near got the firm sued, but the boss stepped in and saved the day. Karim was told he had ten minutes to leave the building.

Karim scratched his head. He knew Lisa would never allow JaQuan to borrow her car. The boy didn't even have a driver's license.

"Senior, do you remember about what time it was that he gave you the ride?"

"Graveyard, Dad. 'Bout two, maybe three. I had to get some castor oil 'cause my stomach was bubbling something bad, Dad. I damn near blew . . ."

Karim pulled off without waiting to hear the rest of Senior's nastiness.

He could hear the laughter the minute he walked into his house. He slowly closed the door behind him.

He walked down the hallway toward his den, where he had a large plasma-screen television, PlayStation, video games, and framed autographed football jerseys. The noise got louder. He stood in the doorway and waited for a second. No one noticed him.

JaQuan was sitting on the sofa playing video games with another boy, who had long, dirty dreadlocks with gold tips to match his gold teeth. A third guy was sitting in Karim's leather recliner with his feet kicked up. He looked like he was fresh out of prison, in a khaki suit complete with a set of numbers stenciled across his left breast pocket. Mr. Jailbird was rolling a blunt as if he didn't have a care in the world. As if he paid the bills.

Dreadlocks looked up and saw him. He casually nodded his head as if to say "what's up."

Jailbird looked up but didn't bother to nod a greeting. He just went back to doing his rolling.

Karim didn't say a word; he just stood there.

JaQuan looked at him. He seemed to have made a decision right then and there that he was going the thug route.

"I think it's time you young men leave," Karim said.

Dreadlocks looked at him as if Karim couldn't be talking to him and went back to playing the game. Jailbird actually chuckled before he moistened the tobacco paper holding the marijuana by running it across his tongue.

"Maybe y'all didn't hear me, but I said its time y'all get the fuck out of my house," Karim barked.

That got their attention.

Dreadlocks tossed the remote on the sofa before jumping to his feet.

Jailbird wasn't so quick to move. He finished preparing his blunt, coughed, and ran his hand over his raggedy beard before he stood. He casually tossed the blunt on the sofa beside JaQuan and lazily walked over to grab his coat, which was sitting on a chair.

"You need to calm down, cuz'," Jailbird said as he passed Karim.

It took every ounce of resolve Karim could muster not to knock the kid's head off. Instead, he walked over, picked up the blunt, and followed the two thugs out of his house.

"I believe this belongs to you," he said, snatching Jailbird by his arm.

Jailbird jerked away and turned an angry glare at him.

For a second, neither of them blinked.

"Trust me, playa. This ain't what you want," Karim said with a smile.

Jailbird looked him up and down with a mean mug before walking out of the house.

Karim watched them as they made their way down his street. He pulled out his cell phone and called the police to alert them of the two derelicts walking around with illegal drugs on them.

Once he was done with his call, he turned on his heels and hurried back to where he'd left JaQuan.

JaQuan jumped to his feet as if he was ready to throw him down.

"This is not a game you want to play," Karim said.

"Whatever, man," JaQuan snapped. "I'm tired of you, Unk. I mean, who you think you is? You ain't my daddy."

"You daddy ain't your daddy. Now, I've opened up my home to you and this is how you gonna act. Look around," Karim said. "This is not the projects and you will not come in here with all that ghetto shit disrespecting my home."

"I ain't asked to come here."

At six feet three inches tall, Karim towered over his nephew, who was just over five foot ten.

"You're a kid; you don't have a choice."

"I'm not like you. I don't wanna be like you," JaQuan said, looking Karim up and down.

"So you see the suit and tie and chalk that up to being soft, hunh?"

"Whatever, man. Just do you and let me do me."

"You know, a part of me said to kick your sorry ass out of my house. Let you be the fake thug you're dying to be, but I know how that story ends and I don't want that for you. The other part of me says you're just stupid. To ignore your ignorance and help you get to where you need to be. But I'mma tell you one last time that I'm not playing games with you. You stole Lisa's car last night," Karim said, taking his suit jacket off. "And I hate a thief, so being that I invited you into my home and you insist upon being disrespectful, I'mma fuck you up."

Karim punched his nephew in the chest and knocked him back into the bookshelf. JaQuan grimaced and grabbed his chest as hardcovers and paperbacks alike came tumbling down on him.

"See, you gonna learn," Karim said, stalking his nephew. "There are consequences for your actions."

He punched JaQuan in the face so hard he thought he broke the boy's cranium.

JaQuan fell down, gasping for air. He covered his head to stop the pummeling.

"Nah. We just getting started, bad-ass," Karim said, walking over to him and pulling him to his feet.

JaQuan covered his face, but Karim punched him in the stomach with enough force to knock Tyson out.

JaQuan screamed in agony.

"Oh, don't scream now. See, if you had your ass in school,

you wouldn't be here getting fucked up now, would you? You scream like that in jail and somebody gonna put something in your mouth."

"Please, Unk," JaQuan said, cowering in the corner.

Karim was about to punch him again but he stopped.

"Why you always sweating me?" JaQuan said, his voice cracking from crying.

" 'Cause that's what you need, got damn it. You are undisciplined and I'm changing that right here and right now." Karim reared back for another punch, but JaQuan fell to the floor and covered his head.

"Get up and sit your ass down in that chair," Karim said, walking over and unplugging the video game. He took the cord and wrapped it up.

"You don't have to like me," Karim said. "But you *will* respect me. Now the first lesson in being a man is learn how to respect other men. Get dressed, damn it. You're going to school."

"Whatchu know 'bout me?" JaQuan screamed. "Whatchu know, Unk? I done been through hell and you don't even know it. Seven years ago. Seven years ago! Do you remember?"

"Remember what?"

"I called you and told you that nigga my momma had staying with me was a freak. He made me do things, Unk," JaQuan said, tears flowing like a river. "And I called you, and you said I was making things up and that I needed to be a big boy. Well, big boys don't get fucked in the ass, Unk. Do they? I wasn't making things up, Unk. He molested me and y'all

ain't do shit. Y'all didn't believe me. Y'all didn't believe me."
JaQuan broke down.

Karim's heart broke into a million little pieces. His eyes
were a river of tears. His legs felt weak and his hand shook at
the revenge he was plotting in his head. He walked over and
sat down beside his nephew. He wrapped his arms around
him and held him as tight as he could.

19

Nadiah tipped the cabbie ten dollars and stepped out of the cab. She waved good-bye to the guy and walked into the house. She wondered why all of the lights were out but thought nothing of it as she flipped the switch, illuminating the room.

She didn't hear any voices in the back of the house, which was abnormal for a Friday night.

Maybe Momma Mae had got tired of everybody and put 'em out. That was known to happen on occasion. She locked the front door behind her. She went to her room and dropped the bag filled with Destiny's gear in the closet.

The house seemed far too quiet. No television blasting, no arguing in the back. Something didn't seem right.

"Momma," she called, walking to the back room where Momma Mae slept.

Nothing.

She frowned and opened the back door.

Nothing.

She closed and locked it.

She walked back into the house.

"Momma," she called again, but the house was empty. "Momma."

Now this was strange.

Momma Mae hardly ever left the house. As a matter of fact, with the exception of an occasional doctor's appointment, she never stepped a foot off of the premises of 324 South Vain. She had people do all of her liquor runs, and either Nadiah or Karim took care of the grocery shopping.

Nadiah checked the bathrooms, all the while calling for her grandmother. "Momma, where are you?"

She walked over to the side of the bed to pick up the phone and dialed Karim's number. The phone rang but no one answered. She walked over and looked out the window, wondering where her grandmother could possibly be.

Maybe she had met some man?

Nadiah smiled at the thought.

Nadiah turned to put the phone back on the hook and looked into the eyes of a deranged man.

Her heart hit the floor. Fear like she'd never felt paralyzed her body. She tried to scream, but no words escaped her lips.

"We gonna get married," Nick said.

The whites of his eyes were showing and he was sweating profusely. He had on a white dress shirt, but it was unbuttoned and speckled with bloodstains.

Finally the piercing scream came from Nadiah. She kneed him in the balls and ran from the room.

Nick leaned over for a minute. Then he gave chase.

Nadiah ran into the bathroom and slammed the door shut.

For a moment there was silence. Then Nick calmly knocked on the door as if nothing were out of the ordinary about his being in the house.

"You don't have to worry, baby. I won't hurt you," Nick said. "I love you."

"How did you get in here?" Nadiah screamed.

No answer.

"Leave, Nick!" Nadiah yelled.

"I can't do that. I love you, girl. I want us to be together. Open the door so we can talk. Now I already told you I ain't gon' hit you no mo'."

Nadiah turned to open the window but stopped when she saw Momma Mae's shoe. It was hanging on the edge of the bathtub.

Nadiah pulled the shower curtain back and saw Momma Mae lying in the tub, her housedress soaking wet and twisted all about.

"Momma," she said with her lip trembling.

The bathroom door flew open and Nick came barreling toward her.

"What have you done to my grandmother?" Nadiah yelled at the top of her voice.

"Na na na na. Dat old woman is the reason why we ain't together. Just listen to me."

"Nick," Nadiah said, trying her best to maintain some sense of control.

"I love you, girl. Now all I want is for us to be together. Let's leave all the foolishness behind."

Nadiah decided to shift gears. She could always control the way their conversations went. "I love you too. I just needed some time."

The shift caused Nick to take a step back.

"But you didn't have to hurt my momma," Nadiah said.

"She tried to shoot me. I came over here to talk to you and she tried to shoot me."

"So you killed her?" she said, her voice breaking as she spoke.

"I didn't . . . ," Nick said, looking at the old woman.

Nadiah looked on the sink's counter and saw Momma Mae's false teeth soaking in a jar of denture cleaner.

The second Nick looked, she grabbed the jar and tossed it in his eyes.

He screamed and grabbed his eyes.

Nadiah ran.

She headed for the front door but just as she unlocked it, Nick grabbed her by her Afro and slung her down to the floor.

"Oh, you trynna play me," he said, rubbing his eyes but still holding on to her. "Got damn it, don't play with me. I been trynna be nice to yo' ghetto ass and this how you gonna do?"

The front door flew open.

"Nigga-ro, have you lost your everlasting mind?"

Nadiah recognized the voice.

"Don't wanna have to put something on ya ass up in here," Monroe, the neighborhood bum, said.

"Old man, you better mind your business," Nick said, releasing Nadiah and approaching Monroe.

"Uh-oh." Monroe's eyes bulged as the hulking black man came toward him. He looked torn. It was as if he was saying, "I know I can't handle this young buck but I can't leave this girl."

"Make ya' move, ya' ugly muthafucka," Monroe said, jumping into fighter's stance.

Nick pulled his leg back and stomped Nadiah in her chest.

"Do something," he barked at Monroe. "I'll kick this bitch whenever I feel like it. Now do something!"

Nadiah fell back, holding her chest.

"Na, you don't want to be treating no lady like that," Monroe said, looking like he was about to cry himself.

Nick grabbed Nadiah by her hair and balled up his fist. "You better raise your ass up outta here, old man, before I stomp a mud hole in your ass."

Boom.

A gunshot blasted, shaking the entire house.

JaQuan stood in the hallway with the smoking gun still in his hand. His eyes were cold as steel.

Nick fell face forward onto the living-room floor.

For a minute everything went silent.

"JaQuan," Nadiah said after gathering herself.

His eyes were fixed on the man lying facedown on the floor. The white shirt was now a crimson red.

Nick wasn't moving.

"Oh God," Nadiah said. "Call 911. Momma needs an ambulance."

Monroe ran to the phone.

Nadiah walked over to JaQuan. She reached out for the gun.

"Give me the gun," she said. "He can't hurt us."

JaQuan was calm as a sleeping baby. He looked down at Nick. He had finally gotten his justice on the man who'd taken away his innocence.

"They on the way," Monroe said.

Nick rolled over on his side. "Aughhh," he moaned in pain.

JaQuan tried to use the gun again but Nadiah grabbed it. "No," she said.

"Move, Ma," JaQuan said. "You have no idea what that faggot is about. I wasn't lying when I told you what he did. I wasn't lying."

Nadiah's eyes widened. Was JaQuan saying what she thought he was saying?

Her hands started shaking. "Give me the gun," she said.

JaQuan must have seen the look in his mother's eyes and held the gun away.

Nadiah rushed Nick and started stomping him with as much force as she could. "You touched my son. I'll kill you," she screamed.

"We gotta get her, J-man," Monroe said, rushing over and pulling Nadiah away from a sure murder charge.

Nick tried to cover himself and hold the bloody bullet hole in his shoulder.

"That li'l nigga lying," he managed.

This time JaQuan needed to be restrained. He started stomping the man with his size-twelve boots.

"Oh Lord," Nadiah said, turning and running to the bathroom.

"That's enough, J-man." Monroe pulled JaQuan away from the beaten Nick.

Momma Mae was conscious and trying to get out of the tub. Nadiah rushed over and helped her. She sat her down on the seat of the toilet.

"Momma," Nadiah said, her heart fluttering a million beats per second. "Are you okay?"

"That boy broke in here. Call the police," Momma Mae said, holding her heart.

"They're on their way," Nadiah said, kneeling down and hugging her grandmother. "Are you okay?"

"I can't breathe too good."

"Oh my God."

"Get me some help, baby."

Nadiah held her grandmother until she heard the wailing of the ambulance.

Twenty minutes later, Momma Mae would be lying in a hospital with tubes everywhere.

20

Karim sat on a plush leather sofa in a swank hotel staring out at the beautiful Atlanta skyline. The view was nothing short of spectacular.

Those long, sexy legs were sitting across from him and he had the best of both worlds.

Mariah smiled.

"Thanks for coming," Karim said.

"Thanks for calling."

"So can you keep a secret?"

"I'm a lawyer; I'm bound by the law to keep a secret."

"That's good."

"Anything and everything we say or do between these four walls is strictly confidential," Mariah said.

"That's good to know."

"Are you ready?"

"Just like that? No foreplay?" Karim said with a chuckle.

"Where would you like to start?"

"You tell me. This is your show; I'm just a bad boy headed to the big house."

"I hear you got fired."

"I did."

"Why?"

"Dropped the ball on this big acquisition."

"Why?"

"Can't seem to shake this funk. I mean, I damn near killed my kid the other day. I gotta do something. I've been drinking like a sailor and I don't even like alcohol."

"Are you an alcoholic?"

"Nah."

"Okay." Mariah nodded, then wrote something on the pad she held on her lap. "So why do you need a lawyer? Sounds to me like you need a counselor."

"I probably can use both. But the lawyer is a little more pressing right now," Karim grunted.

Poor Lisa. Poor Dominic, he thought, and just the thought of being away from his son ate him alive.

"My life is crazy. It always has been," Karim said.

"How so?"

"My grandmother, who raised us, is fighting for her life right now."

"What happened to her?"

"She was attacked in her home by my sister's boyfriend."

"Oh no. Is she okay?"

Karim hunched his shoulders.

"Are your parents still with us?"

"Nope. My brother is gay and my father didn't like that. So he took it upon himself to try and beat the gayness out of him. My mother didn't take too kindly to her son getting abused for being himself. Guns came out, everybody lost. That's the story of my life."

"Murder-suicide?"

"Nah, Mom killed Pops. Got off in the kangaroo courts and died a year later of a broken heart. Heavy price to pay for one man's homophobia if you ask me."

"That's an understatement," Mariah said in disbelief.

"Yeah, it seemed like that incident set the tone for how we handled our problems."

"With violence?"

Karim nodded.

"You seemed to have overcome that. I mean, you're successful. Where is the depression coming from?"

Karim didn't answer. God, this was killing him.

"My nephew came to live with me. He's misdirected, spoiled, and undisciplined, but there's a lot of good under all of that. He has a pure heart. Wouldn't hurt a fly, but four days ago, he shot a man."

"Are you serious?"

"Yeah," Karim said.

"Is he incarcerated? Did the man die?"

"No and no. Neighborhood guy took the rap. Told the cops he was the shooter."

"Okay," Mariah said.

"I just got him back in school and his first week was a good one."

"So is the neighbor in jail?"

"No. My sister's old boyfriend broke into the house. He's the one who attacked my grandmother. She had a heart attack because of it. From what I understand, he was beating my sister up when my nephew shot him. He wasn't even supposed to be there. I let him go to his high school football game, but somehow he ended up over there." Karim shook his head. "This is one time I'm glad he didn't listen. God only knows what that fool would've done if JaQuan didn't shoot him."

"So is this the cause of your stress? Is this the thing that has you seeking solace in the bottle?"

"Nah. I'm not mad at him for that one."

"So why did you call me? I'm still trying to figure out why you think you need a lawyer."

"My brother. That's why I called you. He's the one who keeps me up at night. He's in prison for murder but he didn't kill anyone. I did."

21

"I can't stand niggas," Karim said. He and Omar were riding around asking questions about the people who murdered his son, and they were getting nowhere fast.

"You telling me," Omar said. "I can't believe how people are acting like this is no big deal. They gonna just let a murderer run free because they think they'll be labeled a snitch. That stop-snitching crap is about the dumbest shit I ever heard. Let somebody do something to me, I'm telling. Damn that."

Karim and Omar must have knocked on every door, peeped under every rock, and looked into every set of eyes to ever visit the projects trying to gather information on the killers. After a few days of pounding the pavement, they started getting bits and pieces of info here and there, but nothing major. Then, like an angel in the night, an old man with a long white beard walked up to Karim and handed him a sheet of paper. "This who you looking for. Keep ya' mouth shut 'bout where you got that. People die for less," he said before walking off.

Karim called the police and gave them an anonymous tip about his findings. They told him he needed more evidence. That he needed physical evidence, and they couldn't just barge into a place and arrest someone on word-of-mouth information.

"Can you believe those lazy-ass bastards?" he said, hanging up the phone.

"Yeah. Cops are lazy, man."

"We did all of the work for 'em. I guess we got to prosecute them too."

"Fuck that. Let's execute they asses," Omar said. "Let's make sure they don't run over nobody else's child."

Karim thought long and hard. Every since that day he saw his son Ziar's lifeless body, he'd dreamed about what he would do if he ever found the guys responsible for taking his kid's life.

"You're right. They gotta die."

They located the address the old man had given them, a raggedy little garage in College Park. The guys he was looking for were chop boys, guys who stole cars, chopped them up for the parts, and sold them on the black market.

Karim and Omar did a dry run the day before. They came up with their plan after peeping out the layout of the garage.

They pulled into a vacant lot across the street.

"You sure you wanna do this?" Omar said, now sweating bullets. "I mean, this might've been a bad idea."

Karim, who was calm as the night, nodded his head. He was a soldier on a mission.

"It's already done," he said.

"Be careful, boy," Omar said, handing his brother a big black gun. "I'mma stay here and look out."

Karim looked into his brother's eyes. He loved his big brother. He always had his back. He reached over and hugged Omar.

"I love you, man," Karim said, exiting the car.

"Hush your mouth," Omar said. "I better see you in five minutes. Don't be in there fucking around. Do what you gotta do and get yo' li'l narrow ass back here."

Karim nodded and hustled across the street. He ran up to the side of the building and found the door. He looked through the window, then eased inside.

He heard laughter. He pressed his back to the back wall as his heart rate increased. How could they find humor in anything after what they did? he wondered. Heartless bastards.

He counted the voices and came to the conclusion that there were two guys inside. He took soft steps so he wouldn't be heard. He looked around and found his enemies.

Two men, a fat one with braids and a skinny one with a bald head, were seated at a table counting money. They were laughing like the world was their oyster.

Karim recognized the fat one.

When they saw Karim with his gun drawn, they jumped and reached for their guns.

Boom, Karim's gun blasted into the wall over their heads.

They froze.

Karim walked up to them. Stacks of dollars were on the table.

"You got it," the fat one said, pushing the piles of money toward Karim.

"I don't want your money."

"Th-th-th-the . . . then whatchu want?" Fat Boy stuttered.

Karim stood about five feet away from them.

"Fuck what he wants. Nigga, you need to raise your ass up outta here," Baldy said with a menacing stare. He didn't seem scared. It was as if he had faced the barrel of a gun before.

Karim didn't budge. He was petrified, but revenge is a powerful emotion.

Just looking at them made his blood boil. Both of them had gold teeth and tattoos all over their bodies. The fat one appeared to be in his early twenties, maybe late teens. Baldy looked to be in his early to mid-twenties. Both of them personified the thug life. A life he despised.

"Y'all killed my son," he said calmly.

"Church Boy, you better get your ass up outta here while you still can," Baldy said as he got to his feet.

Karim's eyes turned to slits. All he could see was his lifeless child dangling from his mother's arms and the black Mercedes speeding away from the scene.

"Ho-ho-ho-hol-hold up, shawty," Fat Boy pleaded. "Y-y-y-you got da-da-da-da wrong cats."

Karim pointed the gun at Baldy.

"W-w-w-w-wee weee we ain't d-d-d-d-did sh-sh-sh-sh-shiii-iit," Fat Boy said, on the verge of tears.

"Black Mercedes. Bowen Homes. Six months ago. Yeah, I recognize you," Karim said, eyeing Fat Boy.

A tear made its way down his cheek. "M-m-m-man, please, I-I-I-I'm telling you, you got the wrong . . ."

Boom.

Karim shot Fat Boy right in the center of his forehead. The bullet sent the man-child slamming back into the wall, killing him instantly.

Karim didn't feel a thing.

Baldy took advantage of Karim's desire to see the killer of his son fall, and quickly rushed him. Karim dropped the gun but grabbed on tight to his attacker. He lifted the skinny guy off his feet and slammed him headfirst onto the concrete. It was a violent collision between flesh and concrete. Baldy rolled over onto his back with an agonized grimace on his face.

Omar walked in and ran over to his brother.

"You okay?" he asked in a panic.

"Not yet," Karim said, going after Baldy.

"We gotta get the hell outta here," Omar said.

Karim dropped to his knees, straddling Baldy. He placed his hands around his neck and tightened his grip.

"You sorry muthafucka. You killed my baby," Karim cried as he choked the man.

Baldy's eyes grew wide.

Karim squeezed tighter.

Baldy's veins popped up in his forehead.

Tighter.

Baldy's body started convulsing.

Tighter.

Foam flowed from the corners of Baldy's mouth. His tough-guy persona was long gone. His eyes begged for mercy.

Tighter.

Then he lifted the man's head up and slammed it on the concrete until there was no more resistance.

Baldy didn't fight anymore. The foam stopped; the body went limp. He was dead.

Sirens wailed off in the distance.

"Come on, man," Omar pleaded. "We gotta go."

Karim held on, making sure his son's killer would never kill again.

"He's dead," Omar said, pulling his brother from the deceased thug. "We gotta go."

Karim stood and looked down at the lifeless body. His eyes shifted over to Fat Boy and once again, he felt nothing.

22

Karim stared at Mariah. She looked like she couldn't believe the man sitting in front of her was capable of such violence.

"So how did your brother end up in prison?" she asked.

"Police surrounded the place. They were Johnny-on-the-spot that day. Omar told me to go and hide and walked out with his hands in the air as if he'd done the killing. I was scared. I found the attic and stayed there until the place was empty. Ten hours I stayed up there."

"Seems like the police should've known based on the fingerprints on the gun that it wasn't him."

"I picked the gun up and took it with me. Wiped it down and buried it. Went back a few months later and took it to a guy and had it melted down for scrap metal."

"Why did Omar take the rap for you?"

"He loves me. I'm his little brother and that means something to him. He'll tell you it was because it was his idea, but I would've carried it out anyway."

"So he's sitting in prison because he loves you. I mean, I love my sister, but I'm not going to jail for her."

"At the time I was a freshman in college and Omar had already had his share of trips to jail. He told me he was dabbling in drugs, among other things, so I guess he figured his life was worth a little less than mine."

"Hmm. Interesting. So why now? Why after all this time you now decided to do something to change his situation?"

"I'm getting older and I see the world a little different now. I can't live like this anymore. I gotta tell the truth. My brother's life is not worth less than mine, and it's time he comes home. He's been gone for over ten years."

"So after all this time, how do you feel about what you did?"

"Oh, I have no regrets. Fuck them. I believe the world is a better place. I think I served the black community well."

"Okay. That's all I need to hear," Mariah said, writing on her pad. "I'll be in touch."

Karim stood, then reached out and shook Mariah's hand.

"Thanks. When will I hear from you?"

"Soon. Don't you talk to anyone else until you hear from me, okay? Understand?"

"Yes, ma'am," Karim said with a smile. He glanced around the room. "This is a nice place. But why are you living in a hotel?"

"This is corporate housing for the firm. I'm still looking for a place of my own."

"Damn," Karim said, looking around at the five-star hotel. "I should've gone into law."

"It's not all it's cracked up to be, but I'm very good at what I do. Trust me, you're in good hands."

"That's good to know."

Nadiah walked around the big house in awe. The twentieth-century Victorian rested in the Grant Park section of Atlanta and had character. Twenty-foot-high ceilings, crown molding in every room, oak wood floors, and more fireplaces than she could count. She thought Karim was living well, but this guy's house made Karim's look like a homeless shelter.

"So why aren't you married?" she asked as she took a seat on the softest sofa she had ever felt.

"Why is that the first question out of women's mouths when they come here?"

"Because you have all of this, seems like you'd like to share it with someone."

"No time for it," Victor said. "I have my hand in too many different pots right now. What woman is going to put up with a man who doesn't have time to take her out on a decent date?"

"One who understands the big picture."

"Haven't met that one yet. So are you ready?"

Nadiah had to force herself to keep from trying to dig deeper into his personal life, because she had done this song-and-dance before. The next thing you knew, she would be talking on the phone with him, then dating him, and finally moving her and JaQuan's things into his place. Nope. Not this time. Forcing the issue with a man just because he had the accoutrements of success was a thing of the past. But damn, it was never like this. She could see herself making this place her home.

"As ready as I'll ever be," Nadiah said, standing and brushing a piece of lint off her brown pants suit. She walked over to the area where she was to be photographed and took a seat on the chair.

Victor checked his lighting meter, then started snapping away.

"You look fabulous in brown."

"Thanks."

"How tall are you?"

"Five-eight."

"My sister got the book. She's almost done reading it. She said it's pretty good."

"Really?" Nadiah said, excited to finally hear some feedback on her work. "What did she say?"

"Just that it was a good book. She said she thinks you got something on your hands."

"Are you kidding me?"

"No," Victor said, snapping away. "I haven't had time to even download the file, never mind read it. I can't wait to get into it, though. See where ya' mind is."

"Well, take your time. The words will be the same when you get around to it."

"So tell me, why do you hate men?" Victor said out of the blue.

Nadiah smiled and stopped posing. Victor kept snapping.

"Who said I hated men?"

"Nobody, but your actions speak volumes."

"Well, first of all, I don't hate men. I love men. But I'm not feeling y'all right now. I need some me time."

"That's cool. Me time is good. But why aren't you feeling us right now?"

"Long story, but the short version is: I've been lied to, cheated on, harassed, hit, and lied to. Did I say that one already?"

"You did. I'm sorry you allowed yourself to go through all of that."

"What do you mean 'allowed myself'?"

"Did anybody force you to deal with the person or people who lied, cheated, harassed, and hit you?"

"No, but it's not as simple as you're making it out to be."

"Sure it is. That's why I'm single. When I see character flaws that I'm not willing to deal with, I'm out."

"If everyone took that attitude, then nobody would get married. Some things you just gotta work out or overlook. Not making excuses, but you know."

"Yeah, but you gotta like more about a person than you dislike, and if the one thing you dislike is unacceptable then it's time to keep it moving. But for the record, all men don't lie and harass, and certainly a real man wouldn't hit a woman. So you shouldn't hate all men."

"I don't hate all men, I just don't trust y'all asses." She smiled. "I hate being that way, but outside of my brothers I don't know any good ones."

"Maybe it's all perception. You try to find the good in your brothers, but in everyone else you seek out the bad."

"I don't seek out the bad. But I gotta be careful."

Victor changed the lighting. He moved Nadiah to a different spot and kept snapping.

"You weren't careful with me. You were a downright misandrist."

"A what?"

"Misandrist. That's a woman who hates men." Victor smiled.

"Did you make that up?"

"Nah, look it up."

"I never heard that before."

"It's a word. I looked it up when I first met you," he said, putting his camera down. "That oughta do it. I'll get you a stat sheet in a few days and you can pick the one you like. Do you have a cover designer?"

"Yeah, me. I told you I was an artist. You should let me do a painting for you. That wall needs something," Nadiah said, pointing at a big blank wall in the living room.

"Let me see some of your work and I'll see."

"Really?"

"Yeah. If it's nice, I'll buy a piece from you."

Nadiah went and retrieved her purse. "I don't have a port-folio yet, but I have them on my phone. You wanna see 'em?"

"Yeah."

Nadiah flipped open the phone and went to her photo album. There was a picture of a woman crying while washing dishes. One of a man in a business suit swinging a sledgehammer. A child hiding behind his father's leg.

"That one. I want that one. How big is it?"

"Maybe thirty-six by thirty. It'll fit nicely on that wall once it's framed."

"How much?"

"I don't know. Never sold anything before. Make me an offer."

"I'll give you five hundred for it."

Nadiah was stunned. She had never thought that anything she created would be of any value to anybody other than her. She felt herself getting lightheaded.

"Make it eight," she said with a smile.

"Six."

"This is crazy. Are you serious?"

"Yeah, the picture is nice."

"You are like the angel of good news. I mean, my book, then you buy a picture. Okay, what's the catch?"

"No catch. You are talented and you should be compensated. The picture will look good right on that wall, like you said."

"That's a nice little chunk of change you trynna pay."

"Well, it caught my eye right away. Let me see the rest of them."

They scrolled through several more pictures.

"You do good work. You should put on a show. Let the world see the talents of Nadiah the misandrist."

"Stop calling me that."

Victor smiled. "Let me clean these backdrops up. You can have a seat in the living room."

She did, and he spoke from the den area where he'd taken the pictures.

"You wanna go get a bite to eat?" he asked.

"No, I gotta get back to the hospital."

"It's supposed to storm pretty hard this evening," he said. As if on cue, thunder rumbled, followed by the pouring showers.

"And there it is," Nadiah said.

"I can give you a ride to the hospital."

"I'll call a cab. No big deal," she said. She stared out the big window and took in the pouring rain. Something about it always made her sad. Maybe it was because it was a rainy day when her mother killed her father. It was also raining the day Omar was sentenced to all that time.

He walked over and lifted her chin. "Are you okay?"

"I'm fine," she said.

"You sure about the ride thing?"

"Yeah, you've done enough. Besides, I don't want you thinking I'm some freeloading chick."

"Nah, we're good. How is your grandmother doing?"

"She's a fighter, so I fully expect her to beat this."

Victor nodded. He leaned down for a kiss. She turned away. He held up his hand in apology.

Me time. Me time, she thought. *This is the right move, Nadiah.*

"Look, I better be going," Nadiah said, pulling out her cell phone to call her cab. "Thanks for the photos. When would you like to pick up your picture?"

Victor stared at her. It was as if he could read the battle going on within her. He smiled, but she could tell he was disappointed. "Maybe when your pictures come back. I'll pick it up then."

"How long will that be?"

"Two, three days tops," he said, going back over to the den area and starting to take down the canvases he'd used as a backdrop.

Nadiah called the cab and waited. She looked around the house. There was a picture of Victor on the coffee table. He was on a beach, shirtless and holding a little girl. Nadiah stared at the picture. He was so damn fine. He was such a real man, and she couldn't help but be attracted to him.

She looked over at Victor while he worked. He was wearing a pair of black baggy jogging pants and a snug-fitting T-shirt with Jimi Hendrix on the front. As he worked, Nadiah could see his muscles bulge. He also had a nice little bulge jumping around in the front his pants, and she had to force herself not to look. But there was no denying he was turning her on.

"Enough of this. I want you," Victor said, walking over and grabbing her head.

"I want you, too."

Victor rubbed her shoulders with his big, strong hands, then turned her around so her back was on his chest. He held her close. She could feel his manhood rise on the back of her thigh. The thunder roared and the rain pelted the house.

Oh, how she wanted him! This was the first real man she'd ever been this close to. This was the man she'd prayed to God for.

Victor kissed her neck and she could feel the coolness of his breath on her skin. He ran his hands across her breast and she felt herself becoming aroused. She grabbed his hand and held it on her chest. He turned her around until she was facing him and kissed her. This time she didn't resist. His tongue entered her mouth as he ran his hands through her hair. He was so patient and attentive. She felt helpless to stop him. This was not what she needed in her life right now, but her body said otherwise. He pulled his mouth away and unbuttoned her blouse. He was looking at her like he was daring her to stop him. He took her hard nipple into his mouth and sucked it softly. She reached up and unbuttoned his shirt.

A smile creased his face.

Hers, too.

She took his shirt off, and muscles were everywhere.

Damn, she thought. *Now this is a man.*

Victor eased her over to the sofa and sat her down. He pushed her back while he slid her pants off. She didn't remember him undoing her belt or unbuttoning her pants.

"You're not wearing any panties, little girl," he said.

Nadiah smiled, then frowned as Victor's tongue touched her softest spot.

She moaned.

He played around with her cookie with his tongue, causing her back to spasm. She was so tense. He was her pleasure releaser. He slid his tongue in and out of her. Around her clitoris until she was a river running wild on his tongue. Her body rocked to his rhythm. He stood up and took his pants off. He stood in front of her, waiting. Waiting for her to take him into her mouth. She grabbed his manhood and stroked it. She used both hands. Up and down. He moaned with pleasure. She took him into her mouth until his head snapped back in ecstasy. His eyes rolled in the back of his head.

She was in control now.

"Oh, Nadiah," he said.

He grabbed the back of her head and she reached up and roughly pushed his hand away. He threw a hand up as an apology. He couldn't speak. She held his shaft with both hands and stroked it while she tasted him. Then he pushed her back on the sofa and dropped down on his knees in front of her. He entered her tightness with his thickness and eased inside of her.

She wanted to curse, cuss, and scream all at the same time.

"Oh, Victor," she said. "You ain't right."

He was easing into her slowly, then withdrawing at the same pace. The world was a beautiful place as they found their groove. He pulled out and turned her around. Her nipples stood at attention as he entered her from behind. He reached around and fingered her cookie while he picked up his pace inside of her. Her body bounced back and forth as he pounded her. He was going harder, faster, harder, faster.

"Ohhhh," he moaned as his juices flowed into her.

He collapsed and rested himself on her back. His breathing was heavy. Hers was, too.

"Hello," Victor said, waving a hand in front of her face. "Are you okay?"

"Yeah," she said, snapping her out of her sexual trance.

"Are you okay? I called your name like five times," he said with a smile.

Embarrassed, she wondered if he could tell what she was thinking about.

A horn blew outside and she saw her cab pull up. "Thanks for everything, Victor. Give me a call when those pictures come back."

"Okay," he said, nodding his head.

They shared a quick and friendly hug, and Nadiah felt good about that. He was a total gentleman, and for once she was acting like the lady she knew she was.

24

JaQuan sat in the chair in the corner of the room, playing with his hand-held PlayStation. Over the last week, he'd been spending most of his time at the hospital. He was back in school and getting reacquainted with schoolwork. The thug life was played, and he had his Uncle Karim to thank for opening up his eyes. His so-called boy Marcus had told the police that the drugs he got caught with belonged to him. And when they came looking for him, Karim spoke with them and sent them on their way.

Having his so-called boy play him like that was a hard pill to swallow, but he was glad it happened because it showed him there was no loyalty in the underworld, and that wasn't the kind of life he was trying to live.

"JaQuan, you up?" Momma Mae said.

"Yes ma'am."

"I'm thirsty. Can you get me a drink of water?"

JaQuan jumped to his feet and poured his great-grandmother a glass of water.

"I'm glad you're back in school, chile. Having a education changes things."

"Yes ma'am."

"You momma don't mean no harm. I know you think she don't love you, but she do."

JaQuan nodded his head.

"I'll tell you she loves you 'cause she do. I don't sugarcoat nuttin', and I don't lie. Lying is a sin and I try not to do that. When we found out your momma was gonna have you, we tried to get her to have one of them abortion things 'cause she was so young. Fourteen or fifteen years old." Momma Mae shook her head in pity. "Just a baby herself really. But she wasn't hearing that. She told me if she had to live in a shelter she would, but she was going to have you and she was gonna love you and take care of you. And she tried 'bout everything under the sun to make a life. Made some mistakes, but we all do. You keep on living and you gonna make a whole lot of 'em, too. But God be the judge, not man. Now you running 'round here with your lip poked out mad at her and all she ever did since she was your age was try to make a life for you. She tried to make men your daddy. Now that was wrong, but you were bad as shit. Karim would knock you 'cross your head, but he was always off in school or working. You needed a man in your life. She picked the first halfway-decent fool she saw. But like I said, we all make mistakes. Now I know life ain't been no bed of roses for you, but damn it, be strong. You a man. Forgive your momma, because she loves your little knotty-head self."

"Momma, get you some rest," JaQuan said. "Me and Ma good."

JaQuan had been having sessions with his school counselor about his past, and talking was good. The first thing he had to do was learn to forgive his mother, and he was working on that.

"I'm tired of laying in this damn bed," Momma Mae said. "If it wasn't for that good-looking doctor, I'dda been slipped up outta here."

There was a knock on the door, and in walked a familiar face.

"Nicole," JaQuan said. His smile was as big as Texas. "Whatchu doing here?"

Nicole walked in with a card and a bouquet of flowers.

"I called the house and your mom told me you were up here," she said. "Hi. These are for you," she said to Momma Mae and placed the flowers on the table.

"This my great-grandmamma. Momma Mae. Momma, this my friend Nicole."

"Hey, chile. I didn't know JaQuan had taste. You sho' is pretty. Thanks for the flowers."

"You're welcome," Nicole said.

"You didn't have to come up here in the rain. My mom could've gave you my cell phone number," JaQuan said.

"It didn't start raining until I was almost here," Nicole said. "It's okay."

Momma Mae looked at JaQuan and smiled. "Why don't

y'all go down the gift shop and see if you can find me a newspaper."

JaQuan nodded and they walked out of the room.

They took the elevator down to the first floor, and JaQuan couldn't stop smiling.

"You know your friend Marcus said those drugs belonged to my cousin, don't you?" Nicole said.

"That dude ain't my friend. He tried to say they were mine. I don't mess with him no more."

"That's good. You're better than that anyway. I thought you said you went to Columbia?"

"I lied."

"I know. I got friends over there."

"I use to go there but I got kicked out. I go to Tucker High now."

Nicole frowned and pinched his arm. "You don't have to lie to me, JaQuan. I mean if we're gonna be friends, then you gotta keep it real, man."

"I didn't want you looking at me like I was some kind of dummy. I mean, I was wilding out but I had a lot on my mind. I'm good now, though."

"You sure?"

"Yeah, I'm straight. Did your cousin get out of jail?"

"Yes," Nicole said, shaking her head. "And do you believe she's right back with that clown? If a dude try to lie on me I'm done with him. He can say a pack of bubble gum is mine; if he lying, I'm done."

"I hear ya. So what made you come by here, looking for me? I just don't seem like your type."

"I don't know, and I don't have a type. Like I said, I thought you were cool. Even cooler with that cut," she said, reaching up and touching his closely cropped hair. "It looks good on you."

"I miss my locks."

"Everybody has those. They are played. I like the clean cut better."

"Well hell, if you like it, I love it."

They shared a laugh.

"I might be playing in the game on Friday. Can you get out there?"

"You play football?"

"Yeah. I used to be on the team at Columbia, but then I started wilding out and quit the team. My uncle be tripping so hard at his house. Trynna work me to death like I'm some kind of slave, so I figured I better find something to do at school. That or go home and be Cindafella."

"I didn't know you could get on the team in the middle of the year."

"You can't, but I had a special circumstance because I moved. Coach at my old school called the new coach and they got me on there. So it's on again."

"What position do you play, point guard?"

"I play football, girl," JaQuan said, shaking his head.

"I know. Football players don't have positions?"

"Yeah, but not a point guard."

"Uh-uh, 'cause my uncle played for the Falcons and he was a point guard."

"He might've been a nose guard."

"Yeah, that's it," Nicole said, slapping JaQuan on his arm. "Nose guard."

"Damn," JaQuan said, holding his arm. "You the one wrong and I get slapped. That hurt."

"No it didn't."

"You right, it felt good." JaQuan smiled. "Do it again."

He placed the paper on the counter and paid for it.

"I'll figure out a way to make it to your game. I wanna see what you got."

"I'll see if I can get a touchdown for ya."

"Aww. I'm glad you back in school because I don't want no dummy. Or a weed head."

"All of that is over. It's a new day now."

"Good."

25

Karim sat on the side of the bed and rubbed his son's head while the child slept. His heart cried for what he had to do. But he could no longer look in the mirror and call himself a man if he didn't do the deed.

Lisa walked in the room and paused.

"JaQuan just called. Said he was going to spend the night at the hospital with Momma Mae."

Karim nodded, then looked up at his woman with watery eyes.

"I wish you would talk to me," Lisa said. Her entire body seemed to deflate when she looked at him. "I want to be there for you so bad, but you're keeping me in the dark."

"Sometimes the dark can be a peaceful place."

Karim had never shared a shred of his past with Lisa. As

far as she knew, he was just a regular guy from the 'hood who'd made something of himself. She knew about his dead son and the baby's mother in a mental hospital, but that was it.

Lisa sat on the bed beside him. She placed a comforting hand on his leg and nodded her head.

Six years ago, they met for lunch at a café in downtown Atlanta. Karim had just received his first real paycheck from a real job. He was looking for a new apartment, and Lisa volunteered to help him. They had such a great day. He felt right at home with her. There was something about the smooth cocoa skin and hazel eyes that made him want to keep looking at her. After he found his apartment, she helped him find furniture and decorate. On the day he moved in, she was right there, unpacking boxes and running to Target for the little things like knives and forks. It got late; she fell asleep. When he woke the next morning she was gone. Within only a few short days of knowing her, he realized that he didn't want to be without her. From that day to now, he'd never missed a day of being with her.

Lisa was the perfect woman for him. She was never one to pry and trusted him fully. He never cheated on her and vowed that he never would.

Now he sat there realizing what a grave mistake he had made. She deserved better than him.

"Lisa, I'm not the man you think I am," Karim said with a fluttering heart. "I have to do something that's going to turn our lives upside down."

A concerned look registered on Lisa's face, but she remained quiet.

"When I was eighteen years old . . ." Karim said. His hands were shaking. This was the hardest thing he'd ever had to do. "I made a very bad decision. My brother is paying for that bad decision and I can no longer live like everything is okay."

Lisa jerked her head toward him. She stood and stared down at him.

"The guys who killed my son died by my hands. Omar took the fall, but it was me. All me. He would never hurt a fly and he doesn't deserve to spend the rest of his life behind bars for my stupidity. So what I'm saying is . . ."

Tears formed in Lisa's eyes and her bottom lip started trembling.

"I have to turn myself in."

"No. No. No!" Lisa screamed.

"Lisa," Karim said, jumping up and trying to hold her. She pulled away.

"I will not hear this. You will not leave me to go sit in a prison. You are needed here. Dominic needs you. You're his father. What will he do without you? What will *I* do without you? I mean, Omar . . . I understand what . . . No I don't. You know lawyers. Get one. There has to be a better way. I don't want to hear this," Lisa cried. "People kill people all the time and get off. I mean, isn't there a certain thing called a crime of passion or something? Those guys killed your son! What were you supposed to do? So now they get to kill another one, because Dominic would die without you. I don't know the guys who killed your son, but . . . They are not worth it."

Karim sat back down. His legs were getting weak.

"It's not about them. I'll spit on their graves a thousand times. This is about my brother. He's been in prison ten years for a crime that I committed. I gotta get him out, and the only way I can get him out is to tell the truth."

"So that's it? You just go sign him out of prison and check yourself in? What about us? What about your son? Now I hate to sound mean and selfish but my loyalty is to Dominic and as his father, that's where yours should be, too."

"Lisa, I love you and I love Dominic more than life itself, but how can I teach him to be a man of honor and integrity when I'm a fraud myself?"

"You're no fraud. You're the best father in the entire universe and you cannot—no, you *will* not—take that away from him. What kind of life is he going to have visiting his father twice a month in a damn cage? Come on, there has to be another way."

Karim sat with his head down, staring at his son. Dominic stirred and opened his eyes.

"Tell him," Lisa said. "There he is. Tell him what your grand plan is."

Karim sighed. He looked at Lisa and then back at his son. Dominic crawled into his father's lap and laid his head on his chest.

"Go ahead. Tell him that you'll never be able to read him another bedtime story. That you'll never take him to school again. That you'll never . . ."

"Lisa," Karim snapped.

"Where you going, Daddy?"

Karim turned and looked into his son's almond-colored eyes.

Dominic held his gaze. There was concern in his four-year-old face as if, even at his age, he could sense something wrong.

"Daddy has to take care of some business that might take me away for awhile . . ." Karim said.

"A work trip," Dominic said, rubbing his daddy's face with both hands.

"No. A . . ." Karim started, but Lisa rushed over and snatched the child out of his father's arms.

"You figure out another way," she said with a cold stare. "You will not do this to him."

Dominic cried as his mother took him away. He reached out for his father as he was pulled farther and farther away. That broke Karim's heart.

Lisa rushed from the room. Karim could hear her car keys jingle.

"I wanna stay with my daddy," Dominic said.

"Your daddy has to go be stupid."

He heard the door open, then slam.

Karim couldn't move. He wanted so badly to get up and go after his family but he couldn't move.

26

Karim walked into the hospital room and noticed that everyone else had beaten him there.

"I see the gang's all here," he said, walking over to Momma Mae and rubbing her bruised cheek. "How are you doing, young lady?"

"I'm okay. You should see the other guy."

Karim smiled. He turned to JaQuan.

"You okay?"

"I'm straight," he said, as if shooting a man in the back was just par for the course in the ghetto. "Slept like a baby."

"What about you?" he asked Nadiah.

"I've been better, but things are going to be okay."

"Now that she met another man," JaQuan said, shaking his head.

Karim looked at Nadiah with a big question mark in his eyes.

"It's not like that," she said.

"It never is."

"If you must know, he purchased one of my paintings."

"What paintings?" Karim and Momma Mae asked at the same time.

"I paint. Nice stuff, too. Better than some of the people you have hanging on your walls, big bro'," Nadiah said with a smile.

Karim smiled.

"The man my nosey little son here saw me with is my first client, and I'm not about to let y'all steal my joy with y'all's negativity."

Karim jerked his head back and looked at Momma Mae, who nodded at him as if to say "I guess she told you."

"That's good. I'm happy for you."

"Thank you, Karim," Nadiah said.

"How much he paid you?" JaQuan asked.

"Six hundred dollars," Nadiah said.

"Six hundred dollars? For real, Ma? Buy me some J's."

"Oh, you wanna be my friend now? I'mma J you," Nadiah said. "I got more good news, but I'mma hold off on that for now."

"Yeah, 'cause I'm already sick. I don't wanna keel over and die 'cause Nadiah finally got a clue," Momma Mae said.

"Leave me alone," Nadiah said.

They all shared a few laughs and some small talk before Karim got serious.

"There's something that I need to tell you guys. I've been living a lie."

"You on the down low?" Nadiah asked.

"Nadiah, I'm serious," he said. "I've lived with this lie long enough. It seems that I'm going to be going away for a long time."

Momma Mae tried her best to sit up, but only made it an inch or two before pushing the button to lift her mattress.

"Omar is doing my time. I killed those guys he's in prison for."

"Karim," Momma Mae said. "I know all about what went on. Omar told me all about it. Now if you thinking 'bout doing what I think you're thinking 'bout doing, then you need to let them thoughts alone."

"Momma, this is not a debate. Omar is a human being and he shouldn't be rotting away in prison because of my bloody hands."

"Did you talk to Omar?" Momma Mae asked.

"No. For what? I know what he's going to say."

"Well what about your girlfriend? What about your son? Don't you think you can do them more good home than you could in prison?" Momma Mae said.

"Yeah, but I can't keep Omar locked up. He deserves a life too."

"Karim, this is plain foolishness. Now I want you to go home to your family and leave this mess alone. Omar is okay."

"Why do you guys think Omar is okay with being locked up for a crime he didn't commit? Who would be okay with that?"

"Karim," Momma Mae started. "Omar is . . ."

"What? Gay?"

"No, that's not what I was gonna say. He's where he's happy. He has his little friend and both of them is happy. Now leave it alone."

Karim huffed. He took a long look at his family. Then he walked over and kissed his grandmother on her forehead.

He walked over to Nadiah and she stood. He hugged her and kissed her cheek.

"Karim," Nadiah said with tears in her eyes. "Don't do this. It's not going to make anything better. Omar was out there wilding out. Doing drugs, messing with men. He was probably gonna end up in jail anyway and you know that."

"No, I don't know that and neither do you." Karim backed away from her.

He turned around and stood in front of JaQuan.

JaQuan looked away.

"JaQuan," Karim said. "I'm proud of you, man. You stepped up and you're on your way. I have a lot of respect for you."

Still no words from his nephew.

Karim reached down and rubbed his shoulders before turning away.

"You know what, Unk? I might not be the smartest dude in the world but I sure know stupid when I see it," JaQuan said. "And what you 'bout to do is just plain stupid."

"One day you might understand," Karim said.

"The only thing I understand is you wanna go check yourself into prison and leave little Dominic out here to fend for himself. He might end up like me. You ever thought about that? I hope while you sitting in your cell you cool with that."

Karim listened until JaQuan finished. He took one last look at his family and left the room.

27

Karim sat in his truck. He knew what he was about to do was stupid. It made absolutely no sense, but he couldn't get any peace and he knew none would come until his brother was out of that prison cell. He looked at his mobile phone and noticed he had seven missed calls from Lisa. He knew she was worried sick about him and he hated himself even more for putting her through this. He scrolled through the other calls and stopped when he noticed Mariah's number. He pressed "talk."

"Hello," a soft voice said.

"Can you meet me?"

"Karim?"

"Yeah."

"Meet you where?"

Karim gave her the location and hung up. He put his truck in gear and pulled away.

Twenty minutes later he sat there waiting for Mariah. Maybe she wasn't going to show.

But why would she? He couldn't afford to pay her at three hundred dollars an hour and this was a capital case. Lots of time and energy would be needed to defend him, and if he were to get Omar out he would pretty much have to confess. So what was the purpose?

He put his truck back in gear and drove two blocks over, parking across the street from the jail.

He walked into the building on legs that were like wet noodles.

"I need to see a homicide detective," he said to the desk sergeant.

"In reference to?"

"A homicide," Karim said, looking at the guy like he was clueless.

"Hold on," the sergeant said, picking up the phone. He spoke with someone for a few seconds, then hung up. "Have a seat."

Karim walked over to the seating area and had to restrain himself from getting up and walking out.

What am I doing? he wondered. *This is stupid. Leave, Karim. Just get Omar a new lawyer and leave.*

He stood and started walking toward the door.

"Can I help you?" a tall black guy said. "I'm detective Louis Johnson."

The man reached out his hand.

Karim stopped and stared at the outstretched hand. "Ah, no thanks."

"Sir, if you know something about a homicide, you might want to share it with me."

"I ummm," Karim said, flustered. He didn't know what to do. "I . . ."

He stopped when he noticed Mariah coming through the front door.

"I'm *soo* sorry. I got caught in traffic," she said to Karim. She turned to the detective. "Mariah Waters," she said, handing him a card. "And you are?"

"Detective Johnson. Homicide."

"I'll need a few minutes with my client alone before we speak with you."

Detective Johnson looked confused for a second, then nodded his head. He turned away and walked through the same door through which he'd entered.

"What's up?" she said. "You don't look too good."

"I don't feel too good."

"Let's go somewhere and talk," Mariah said.

Karim looked around, already feeling like a prisoner.

"Come on," Mariah said, grabbing his hand.

They walked outside and found Mariah's car, which was parked down the street.

"Let me get something straight," she said. "You're not trying to go to jail because of some moral obligation to your God or anything. You just want to get your brother out, am I correct?"

"Right," Karim said.

"Okay. I told you not to talk to anyone until you heard from me. Now I've been working on this, though I do have other cases that came before you. But here's what I have. I have requested a new hearing based on exculpatory evidence that shows Omar is innocent. Hairs were found at the scene and not one of them matched Omar's. No murder weapon was ever recovered, so basically they have a confession from a guy high on drugs. As far as you and your brilliant plan go, the law doesn't work that way. You can't just say you did something and go to jail and they let someone else out for it. If that were the case, parents would do it all the time for their children. The State is going to refuse to accept your statement simply because they don't want to admit that they wasted half a million dollars incarcerating the wrong man for ten years. The D.A. is up for reelection and that's not the kind of publicity he needs. So once again, keep your mouth shut. You will stay away from that place," she said, pointing back to the jail. "From what I found, the police did a half-ass job at best, and it's not your job to do theirs. I admire your courage but it's totally unnecessary. Give me a few more days to get some things in place; then I will approach the district attorney with my findings. Getting Omar home won't be easy and it won't happen overnight, but we'll get him home. The burden of proof is not ours, it's on the State, and if they can't justify their conviction—and they won't be able to do it—then he has to be released."

Karim had heard those same words from four different lawyers, but he knew in his heart that Mariah knew what she was doing.

"So what now?"

"Nothing. Let me handle it. I'll be in touch. Go home."

Karim reached over and gave her a hug. "Thanks. I owe you one."

"No, after this one you'll owe me a helluva lot more than one." She winked. "Besides, you still may have to go to prison."

Karim dropped his head as the reality set in.

"But I doubt it. The State won't pursue it any further than they have."

"Thanks, sexy lawyer lady," Karim said. He ran his eyes over those shapely legs once before he got out of her vehicle.

Mariah caught his wandering eye and shook her head. "Men! Here you are about to turn yourself in to prison and you're still being fresh."

"Not being fresh, just admiring a beautiful woman who saved my life. Now let me go home and make two other beautiful people happy." Karim smiled.

"That's true. After that you belong to the homeys."

Karim frowned.

"Go home to your family, Karim," Mariah said with a smile.

Karim exited the car and walked back to his truck. All of a sudden he was okay. For the first time in ten years he felt good about Omar's situation. He finally had a lawyer on the case who knew what she was doing. Those other asses should disbar themselves.

He jumped in his truck and hopped on I-20 East headed back to Stone Mountain.

Twenty minutes later he walked into his house. Lisa and Dominic were kneeling on the sofa as if they were praying.

They turned around when they heard him. Both had tears in their eyes.

He walked over and stopped in front of them.

"Daddy," Dominic said, jumping from his mother and leaping into his father's arms. "Mommy, God works."

Karim smiled and held his son tight.

Lisa's bloodshot eyes found his and he nodded.

"I don't have the ring yet, but if you'll have me, I'd like to be your husband."

Lisa looked at him as if she couldn't be hearing him right.

"God works, Mommy," Dominic said again, his big eyes wide.

"He sure does. We are going to church every day. I prayed to God that He'd place a brain in your head. He must've listened, because here you are."

"We gotta go every day?"

"Every day," Lisa said, running over to her man and collapsing into his arms.

There was a bump against the house.

"What was that?" Lisa asked, startled.

Karim pulled himself away from his woman and walked toward the sound. He peeked out the window.

"What is it, baby?"

"I don't know if I should let you see this or not," Karim said, shaking his head.

Lisa walked over and peeked out the back window.

"Oh my God," she said, covering her mouth.

Senior was outside on their deck wearing nothing but a pair of too-small white underwear.

"Baby, somebody needs to get Senior some help," Lisa said.

"Ain't that the truth?"

The phone rang, and Karim reached over and picked it up. He never said a word. Just dropped the phone and hit his pockets, searching for his truck keys.

"Come on. We gotta go."

"What happened?" Lisa asked.

"Momma Mae just had another heart attack and she's not breathing."

28

"Mable, or should I say Mae, as she was so affectionately known to her friends and family, shot me," Pastor Ford said as sweat poured from his shiny black face in the overheated church. "And I deserved it. But let me tell you another thing. That shot to my buttocks changed my life. If it had not been for Mable Harrison's gun, I might not be standing here right now. I was on a fast track to nowhere. She forced me to slow down. Oh, I tell you, I loved that woman. She was a woman who never met a stranger. And she never had a dime that she wasn't willing to share. If you were in need of something and you went to her, you were no longer in need. I tell you, the good Lord was sho' good to allow us to spend seventy-three wonderful years with this angel of a woman. Her life was a blessing. Her house was always a good place to fellowship and enjoy a few spirits." The reverend smiled, much to the delight of the crowd. "I met Mable when I was in the world. I was running around doing all sorts of the devil's foolishness. Robbing, stealing, doing drugs, and sleeping with white women. Mable shot me and came to the hospital every day to check on me. She made me believe that I was a better man than I was letting on to be. See, sometimes people will see things in you you don't even see in yourself. Mable saw in me that I was a man of God. I'll tell you, when I was laid up in that hospital bed, all I could think of was if God gave me another chance, then I would do right by Him. Now I still visited Mae's on occasion, and every now and then I would partake. See, the Bible don't have a problem with the drinking; it's the drunk. Mable wouldn't allow me to backslide. Oh, I'll tell ya. Mable Harrison was a good woman. Didn't take no mess but didn't give any, either. Always had an easy smile and an open heart. So on this day, I tell you heaven is a little more heavenly on this day," the pastor said to an ovation.

The choir played a few more soulful gospel tunes, then the masses started filing out.

Karim's family and Nadiah and JaQuan loaded up in a limousine and headed out to the burial ground.

Karim sat under the tent in the drizzle wearing a black suit with a black shirt and matching tie. The people were lined up to take one last look at the body of Momma Mae. Nadiah stood before the casket and placed the bound copy of her novel on Momma Mae's chest. She touched her lips, then touched Momma Mae's before taking her seat.

Karim looked around at all of the beautiful black people

who had come to celebrate the home-going of one of Georgia's own. There must have been at least five hundred people there. Blacks, whites, Puerto Ricans, and even the Asian man who ran the check-cashing joint on the corner were in attendance.

JaQuan tapped his leg as the gravesite caretaker closed the casket and placed it in the machine that lowered it into the ground.

"Let's do it, Unk," he said, standing.

Karim followed his lead. They walked over and took the shovels from the men who were hired to cover the casket with soil.

Karim looked over at his nephew and saw white tracks from dried-up tears on his chocolate cheeks.

"You okay?" he asked.

JaQuan nodded his head as he dug up the dirt and tossed it down onto the casket.

"The doctors said she didn't feel any pain. She went in her sleep," Karim said.

"I know. This is so crazy. Ten days ago, she was fussing and cussing and now she's gone."

"No days are promised, nephew. You gotta live your life to the fullest. Never know when your time will come."

JaQuan nodded again.

Nadiah walked over and watched as the only two men in her life covered the woman who had taught her everything.

Karim tossed dirt on his grandmother and realized how truly important family was.

29

One Year Later

It was hot as hell up in Harlem as we navigated our way through the crowded streets, where it was at least a hundred degrees in the shade.

"Man, it's too damn hot for me not to be in Brazil, getting my freak on," Leo said.

"Yo' ass is gonna get them AIDS you keep on sleeping with any and everybody," Nadiah said.

"I won't sleep with nobody else if you start acting right."

"Let it go," Nadiah said.

We were in New York for a joyous occasion and I couldn't have been happier. Mariah had made a few phone calls and got JaQuan's charges dropped.

I looked at him, and he seemed to be a totally different kid than he was a year ago. He had buckled down and taken a few classes in summer school so that he could get back in his correct grade. His entire world consisted of football and that little girl Nicole, who had his nose wide open.

JaQuan looked up and took a picture of the street sign that said "Malcolm X Blvd."

"Come on, boy. Stop acting like a tourist," Nadiah said, looking at her map.

"I *am* a tourist," JaQuan said as he snapped another picture. "What we looking for?"

"The Random House tent."

"It's right there." JaQuan pointed at a green tent with big white letters spelling out RANDOM HOUSE.

"Where?"

"You don't see that big-ass green tent, Ma?"

"Watch yo' mouth boy," I snapped.

"Sorry 'bout that, Unk, but I'm just saying, it's right there."

"Yeah, well, you need to work on that language," I said, giving him a stern look. Damn, the minute I give that boy some credit he goes and cusses at his mom. Well, he's only sixteen, so we got a ways to go.

"Yeah man, what the hell wrong with you cussing in front of your momma?" Leo said. "Do it again and I'mma marry her so I can be your daddy. That way I can whip that ass."

JaQuan chuckled and snapped a few more pictures.

"You think it's funny," Leo said, grabbing JaQuan in a playful headlock.

I shook my head.

Every now and then I would think of where I could be. Where Omar still was, and think how lucky I was.

We walked over to the tent, and books were everywhere. I

saw a big poster of Nadiah's book and I felt a huge sense of pride take over my body. I still couldn't believe this was my little sister.

"Nadiahhhhh," called Brady, a tall white guy who was the lead publicist at Random House and the one responsible for getting her book all the buzz it received. "Glad you could make it!"

"Hi," Nadiah said. "This is my son JaQuan, my brother Karim, and our charity case, Leo," she said with a smile.

Brady smiled. "He doesn't look like a charity case."

"Whatchu trynna say?" Leo said. "You trynna call me fat on the sly?"

"Um, no," Brady said with a little nervous glare. "Well, it's nice to meet you guys," he said, reaching out his hand to everyone. "Nadiah has the hottest book in the city right now. I'm totally psyched about it."

"Are ya psyched?" JaQuan said, making fun.

"It's a classic. I'm Miriam." A pretty brown-skinned woman walked up with her hand extended. "It's nice to finally meet you."

Nadiah and Miriam shared a sisterly hug. "Hey girl," Nadiah said. Then she announced to her family, "This is the lady who purchased the rights to my book."

"Thank ya," I said. "You don't know what you did."

"It's a good book. Are you guys enjoying the city so far?" Miriam asked.

"It's cool," Nadiah said, nodding her head.

"Well, we have you signing here at two, you're on a panel inside the Schomburg at three, and you're doing your other thing tonight at the *Black Issues Book Review* reception at seven. And you're not even on tour yet. Get used to it; your book is hot."

"Man, I'm going to look around," Leo said. "Y'all couldn't find a big building or something with some air conditioner in it?"

"It is hot," Brady said. "Is that your husband?" he asked Nadiah.

"God no. My boo name is Victor. He wanted to be here, but he had to do a photo shoot in Paris for some television show," Nadiah said.

Brady cleaned away some boxes.

"You can get started now. A few people were here already looking for you," he said, pointing at a chair sitting in front of a large stack of her novel, *Momma's a Virgin*.

A fan ran up. "Oh my God. This book is so damn good. Girl, you did your thing with this one. I loved it when the old girl kicked that old pervert in his nuts. Good for him with his old stinking self. I need to get two copies."

I watched my sister as she sat down and signed her books. I was so proud of her. She had been through so much. We all had, but this was good. Good for her, good for our family. It was good for JaQuan to see his mother doing something productive and getting paid for it.

"Look at her, Unk," JaQuan said proudly. "She shining."

Nadiah signed the girl's copies and the line got longer.

"Daddy," Dominic said, running up to me. I scooped my little man up and walked over to the love of my life. "When did you guys get here?"

"Cabs in New York are dangerous," Lisa said. "Congratulations, Nadiah, I'm so proud of you."

"Thanks. Hell, I'm proud of myself, girl. Lisa is the one who edited my book when I first finished it," Nadiah said.

"Great work," Miriam said. "You want a job?"

"No," I said. "We just got married and I can't have my wife in this big city."

"Congratulations," Miriam said. "You guys have the cutest kid."

"You're lucky to have such a supportive family," Brady said, handing out cold bottles of water.

"Yeah, they love me," Nadiah said.

She signed the poster; then it was time for them to head into the museum where she was doing a one-woman art show.

Momma Mae had left her a nice little chunk of change. She spent a large portion of it on a lawyer to try and gain some form of custody of her daughter and spent a little more on her one-woman show.

All of Nadiah's pieces were on display. The place was packed.

People were walking around admiring the work of the hottest author in the country when a loud voice entered the building.

"How in the hell can a momma be a virgin?" a familiar voice said, holding a copy of the novel.

"Omarrrrr!" Nadiah screamed. She stood and almost knocked her fans over as she ran to her brother. "Omarrrrr. You're home!"

"I ain't home, girl, I'm in New York."

I watched my brother as he hugged Nadiah, then Dominic, then JaQuan, then Lisa, and finally me.

For the first time in over eleven years, I was finally at peace.

ABOUT THE AUTHOR

TRAVIS HUNTER, once named Author of the Year by readers of the *Atlanta Daily World,* is the author of *Something to Die For, The Hearts of Men, Married but Still Looking, Trouble Man,* and *A One Woman Man*. Hunter lives in Atlanta. Visit his website at www.travishunter .com.